# FOLLOW

## ME

## LIKE

## ME

## Charlotte Seager

# FOLLOW ME LIKE ME

## Charlotte Seager

MACMILLAN CHILDREN'S BOOKS

*For my dearest great granny, Mary Margurite Gibson (née Wild),*
*and her son, my beloved grandad Papa, Philip Graham Gibson*

First published 2019 by Macmillan

This edition first published 2019 by Macmillan Children's Books
an imprint of Pan Macmillan
The Smithson, 6 Briset Street, London EC1M 5NR
Associated companies throughout the world
www.panmacmillan.com

ISBN 978-1-5290-0206-5

The right of Charlotte Seager to be identified as the

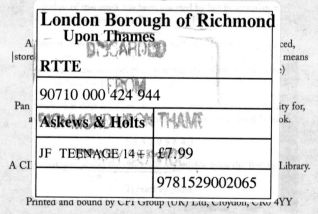

A ... ced,
|store ... means
... )

Pan ... ity for,
a ... ok.

A CI ... Library.

Printed and bound by CPI Group (UK) Ltd, Croydon, CR0 4YY

Visit www.panmacmillan.com to read more about all our books and to buy them.
You will also find features, author interviews and news of any author events, and you
can sign up for e-newsletters so that you're always first to hear about our new releases.

I don't realize I'm trembling until he looks at me. His eyes are so beautiful, pale grey irises speckled with flecks of green. He gazes down at me, smiles, and I feel my whole body melt.

'Here – this is how you do it.' He takes the handle of the rowing machine and expertly pulls it back. The muscles in his arm ripple. I look away, and my cheeks grow uncomfortably hot.

'Now you try.'

I do, but my hands are still shaking, and I can't quite pull it right. I yank the handle, and it makes a loud, jarring screech.

I can feel the heat everywhere now. On my face, my head, my neck.

But when I look up, he's laughing. He takes the handle from me gently, resting a hand on my shoulder. My stomach gives a weird lurch at his touch. His beautiful eyes look down at me, teasing, as though we share a secret.

# CHAPTER 1

## Amber

There's not just one picture of his face – there are hundreds. Scattered around the screen like smiling confetti, lighting up the dark. Football matches, blurred screenshots of drunken, well-thumbed photos. Gently I drag each image into a folder.

As I work, the clock on my bedroom wall gives a low rhythmic tick, but I don't register the sound. It's like the room around me is out of focus. All I can see is his face.

Instagram. Twitter. Facebook. There's also a page on the new 'Trainee Personal Trainers' on the Ferrington gym website. The third one down says *Ren Moore*, and beside a brief description there's a small, blurry image of him. He is seventeen, as I thought, and the description says he's only been training as a personal trainer with the local college for the last month.

I right-click save and drag that photo into the folder too.

My laptop has linked up a slideshow of the images, which I thought would be cringey, but it's actually OK.

Is this confidence-building?

Maybe if I look at him enough, here in my bedroom, I'll stop choking up when I actually see him.

Even thinking about the last time I was at the gym makes my cheeks warm.

For the millionth time, I conjure up the way he gazed at me, his hand gently brushing my shoulder. The tingling feeling that swept through my body.

Did *he* feel it too?

I've replayed that moment so many times, it feels like it should be worn out – but each time I remember it, the memory gets brighter, more vivid.

The photos are playing on a loop, flicking through what looks like his entire life: a school Paris trip; training at the gym; that house party he live-streamed.

My eyes slide across to my own Instagram profile. There isn't really much there to be honest – but then again, I'm not very snap-happy. When I go out . . . Oh, who I am kidding? I have nothing to take photos of.

My twin brother Seb's Instagram page is the polar opposite. There isn't a single of photo of him where he isn't surrounded by friends. We've both only been at this school for six months, but it took him about three seconds to slot into his new surroundings.

But it's OK. We've always been different.

When I scroll back to the slideshow, I'm struck by the curve of his face. His flushed cheeks, beautiful speckled eyes, and that look he gets when he's explaining something and his lips drop open slightly.

If he were right in front of me now, how would I feel?

The slideshow stops on one image. It's of him, topless, posing in the mirror, and it makes me feel incredibly small. There's dark shadows accentuating the curves of his muscles. The angle of his sharp face, highlighting his cheekbones, and he's jutting out his lower lip.

OK, I know it's a bit try-hard. It's actually an incredibly vain photo, and if I knew him better, I'd probably tease him about it . . . But if I can speak to him topless and not completely burn up, maybe I can speak to him properly next time I'm in the gym.

I purse my lips into a funny little smile and whisper, 'Hey.'

I swallow and try again.

'Hey.'

I tilt my head and give my hair a little flick.

'What are you doing here—'

At that moment, a flood of light illuminates the room. My eyes snap open, taking a moment to focus on the lanky frame of Seb, who is bounding through my bedroom door.

I slam my laptop shut, my heart thudding.

'Get out!' I hiss.

'Yo, sis! Guess what Bill and me just saw on—'

He's already heading towards me, laughing, arm outstretched with his phone.

'Get out!' I say, louder this time.

He blinks. 'Whoa – what's wrong with—'

'Just leave me alone! OK? Leave me alone!' I'm shouting now, my face burning.

I'm not sure why my voice is so high, but Seb doesn't need telling twice. He rolls his eyes to the ceiling, muttering, 'Christ,' before doing a loop of my bed and slamming the door shut behind him.

Once he's left, the room falls dark again.

When I open up the laptop, my hands are shaking.

I look down at the hundreds of pictures of Ren, and suddenly I'm struck by the ridiculousness of what I'm doing. I snap the laptop shut and lie back in bed, staring at the ceiling.

Ren is gone. Seb is gone.

My eyes rest on the outline of my hands in the dark.

Alone.

# CHAPTER 2

## Chloe

After school, Louise, Rachel and Ameerah are screaming so loudly, I can't even make out what they're saying.

'This, Chloe – get this!'

Rachel's hands are clutching silky red fabric – a sequinned devil costume that glimmers in the light as she tugs it off the hanger.

I tilt my head to one side. 'It's a little . . . *much*, wouldn't you say?'

Rachel drops it like it's burning her fingertips. 'Ugh, yeah – way too much.'

I turn away, not really paying attention. My eyes have already focused on my phone, which is buzzing incessantly with notifications. In a group chat, a couple of the guys are posting memes about my ex-boyfriend Tom's Halloween party on Thursday, in just over a week's time, and a few more people have commented on my Instagram posts.

I click on the latest photo: me in the mirror, my lips red and slightly parted, body tilted forward, a low-cut grey dress clinging to my waist.

It took me about three hundred photos to get that pose right, to look both thin and curvy, and I'm still not happy with it. My hips jut out too much on one side, and my eyeliner is definitely wonky. Ugh.

There are five new messages, almost all from guys at school. One of them, Sven, I don't know, but I'm pretty sure it's this guy who works in the corner shop near my house. He's been commenting on every photo I post, things like *beautiful* and *stunning*. This time, he hasn't written any words – just posted a mouth-open, shocked-face emoji.

'Chloe! What do you think of this?'

Louise is walking over, brandishing a deep-green slip of velvet. It dips down at the front and is decorated with beaded feathers across the hem. I stroke the material.

'Nice,' I say, taking it off her.

Louise smirks at Rachel and goes back to rifling through the hangers.

I can see myself in this, dressed as a peacock, with shimmery make-up across my face and feathers in my hair. I imagine stepping into Tom's familiar beamed house, passing through that staircase with the crooked bannister. Him glancing at me as I walk in.

Thinking of Tom makes me gnaw the inside of my lip. I'm not angry with him any more – I just feel kind of hollow. I can't stop thinking about the last time I saw him: his ashen face, lower lip sticking out; the way his eyes hardened when I threw my arms in the air and said, 'Maybe we should take a break.' He seemed to have already made up his mind.

8

And I felt so dizzyingly angry then, I wanted to scream at the top of my lungs. Tell him to stop messaging other girls and that he clearly didn't care about me. But I didn't. Instead I rolled my eyes and left. When I said the word *break*, he jolted as though I'd hit him, and I can still remember the weird metallic taste in the back of my mouth as I walked away.

My phone buzzes again, snapping me out of it. I have over a thousand followers now, and pretty much every day there's a new guy who comments on my photos or slides into my DMs.

Sometimes a guy will start following me and then comment or like every single one of my 200 photos, which I find a bit creepy.

But I'm not paying attention to my profile; I'm on Tom's. Skimming image after image that I've seen a million times before (he doesn't post very often). Underneath his most recent post – a photo of him laughing with a couple of friends at the local bar, Playshack – there is something new.

A comment from another Year Eleven girl, Jasmin Reid, who's in my form at school.

**jaz_R** *Looking good* ☺

I stare at it for several seconds.

Christ. What is she playing at? Has he been messaging with her too? We've only been split up for a few weeks – he's just trying to upset me! I click through to Jasmin's page and see Tom has posted a wink emoji on one of her recent photos.

I jut out my chin. Well, two can play at that game. I skim through my recent notifications, trying to find someone Tom doesn't know who has started commenting on my selfies.

There's this Sven. About a week ago, he sent me a DM – *you're the most stunning girl I've ever seen* – though maybe he was drunk, as it was followed by a mishmash of letters. And his Instagram page is odd: mainly photos of him by himself, biking or playing football.

Oh, who *cares*? He'll do.

On one of his most painstakingly posed photos (one arm outstretched behind his head so you can see the muscle of his arm), I click like and type a comment.

**Chlo03** *Bold ;)*

My phone almost instantly lights up with two new DMs.

'Tom will like that dress,' says Louise, suddenly at my side. I lock the screen of my phone. She nods at the material I'm holding. 'Wasn't his favourite colour green?'

At the mention of Tom, all the other girls look at me.

I wrinkle my nose as though trying to remember something.

'Tom? Oh *God*, that feels like a lifetime ago.' I snort a laugh. 'Who cares what he thinks?'

# CHAPTER 3

## *Amber*

The floor-to-ceiling gym mirrors light up every imperfection on my face. There are dark purple rings under my eyes, a sheen of grease across my forehead, and a huge whitehead on the tip of my nose. My fingertips shake slightly as I swing myself onto the exercise bike.

I grimace at my reflection. Oh *God* – I wish I'd had more sleep. I wish I hadn't stayed up until 2 a.m. obsessing about this very moment: being at the gym attached to our school before lessons; the chance of seeing Him again.

What if I mess it up?

What if I say something stupid? Or my voice starts quivering in a dumb, nervous way? Worse: I could try to speak to him, and he could just ignore me completely.

My whole body is trembling now. Little goosebumps are travelling up my arm, and there's a buzzing feeling tickling my skin. I clamp my teeth shut so they don't chatter.

*Enough.* He's not here yet. I need to stop this.

I tug my jumper over my fingertips and start stabbing at the buttons. An ear-splitting beep makes me jump back as the machine turns on.

Did anyone see that? I dare a glance across the room, but no one is paying attention. The man closest to me has headphones in, and the woman lifting weights in the corner is looking directly in the mirror.

I gently start to pedal.

The wheels are spinning, faster and faster. Blood rushes to my face. Ren could walk in. Any minute now.

There's a soft tearing sound and a tug at the bottom of my trousers.

*What the—*

One of the pedals has got caught on a loose thread at the hem of my jogging bottoms. I lift my feet up, but the pedal keeps spinning for a few seconds, winding tighter and tighter against the fabric.

It starts to pull my jogging bottoms down on one side. Glancing round, I yank my trousers up, but they get tugged down again.

I try to manoeuvre my leg away from the machine, but the thread is wound so tightly round the pedal that I'm either going to fall flat on my face or pull my entire jogging bottoms down over my bum.

My cheeks start to prickle.

Oh God. I'm *stuck*.

Out of the corner of my eye, I see a tall guy with a flash of dark hair in one of the royal-blue personal trainer tops. Please, *please* tell me it's not Ren. Don't let him come over.

I try to bend down so I can untangle the thread, but I can't.

12

I'm not flexible enough, and if I bend any further, my trousers are going to come right down.

Tears of humiliation begin to burn my eyes.

This was so pathetic, coming here. Thinking me and Ren would actually speak to each other. Making a slideshow of photos. Now this is what's really going to happen: I'll get stuck on this machine for the entire morning and eventually have to rip my trousers off in order to even make it into school.

Oh God – and I'm not even wearing *nice underwear*.

They're white – and *baggy*. The first thing I grabbed when I got dressed this morning, half asleep.

I blink several times, sniffing back tears.

At that moment, a girl appears beside me. She's tall and thin with wavy thick red hair tied up into a topknot. She's wearing the same royal-blue personal trainer top as Ren's.

'I'm Iulia, one of the trainees here – do you need some help?' She glances down at my snagged trouser leg, then lowers her voice. 'I saw you struggling. Don't worry – I can get it.'

In a matter of seconds, she's kneeling down, deftly unwinding the thread from the machine. At one point, she leans almost to the ground and uses her teeth to snap a dangling thread, setting me free.

I gingerly lift my foot off the pedal. There's no tug. The hem of my jogging bottoms is slightly frayed, but I just feel an overwhelming sense of relief that I'm not going to be glued to the pedal all morning.

'If you need anything else, don't hesitate to ask!' says Iulia, smiling broadly, and I realize with a jolt that she's the first person from school to smile at me all week.

I open my mouth. I want to say something to thank her for

13

getting me out of this, but before I get a chance, she's already leaped off to give a man advice about his squatting technique.

Now my legs are free, I don't want to take any chances. I jump off the machine, gather up my water bottle, and scuttle back to the changing rooms.

Ren is nowhere to be seen.

How could I have been so pathetic? Getting up early and coming here just in case he was working. All the trainee personal trainers are at college and just do placements at our town gym in the leisure centre; they're not even here every day. I'm pretty sure Ren finished school last year, so he's just a year older than me. But maybe he still thinks I'm some stupid little kid, coming in here from the school gates next door, changing into my PE gear.

In a way, maybe it's good he's at college today. What would have happened if Iulia hadn't freed me? I could have ended up showing my bum to the entire gym.

I almost feel like crying again as I pull my school jumper roughly over my gym shirt. I'm an idiot, aren't I? That smile he gave me obviously meant nothing to him. I shouldn't have come back here. It was completely and utterly stupid.

At the main entrance to the leisure centre, two receptionists have their heads together and are whispering. I don't pay them much attention; my mind is circling with horrible thoughts about what Ren thinks of me. Thoughts like glue that stick to my mind and won't budge, no matter how hard I try to shift them.

'I can't believe it about Ren!' hisses the male receptionist.

My feet suddenly stop working. I pretend to find something in my gym bag.

'That manager always had it in for him.'

14

I drop my bag. The two receptionists glance over at me.

*Did they hear me?*

'Do you need any help, sweetie?' says the woman, leaning over the desk.

I snatch up my bag. 'Um, no, I'm fine,' I say, then hurry out of the double doors.

The cool wind hits my cheeks, but I ignore it.

Ren? *In trouble?*

I remember the way he smiled at me. His kind eyes. How he helped me use the machine the first time I went to the gym, when I was so unbelievably stupid.

I nibble on the inner corner of my lip.

He wasn't at the gym today. Now I think about it, he's always at the gym when I come on a Wednesday morning.

Something's definitely not right.

What's going on?

Absently, I open up my phone on Ren's social media pages and refresh them a couple of times, but quickly close it again. There's no new posts.

# CHAPTER 4

## Chloe

Later that afternoon I wander into the kitchen clutching the sequinned green dress. Mum is standing with her back to me, facing the mirror. She's wearing a little denim skirt, which would probably be too small for me, and a skin-tight leopard-print top. As she dabs her lips with an Yves Saint Laurent lipstick, her gold bracelets clatter on her scented wrists.

I clear my throat, but Mum doesn't react.

I dump my dress on the island in the centre of the kitchen and get some orange juice from the fridge. As I pour myself some, a droplet spills on the worktop.

'For goodness' sake!' Mum's piercing voice is high and makes me jump.

'What?' I say.

She's facing me now, hands on her hips.

'Do you have *any* idea how much these marble worktops cost?' she says.

'Sorry,' I mutter, grabbing the tea towel and mopping it up.

17

But Mum has stopped talking and is staring at my face with a frown. 'Come here.' She tries to grab my cheek.

'What? No!' I duck away from her.

Mum's brows knit together. 'Is that a spot on your chin?'

'No, Mum. I don't know, OK?'

She pulls up a chair, sits down, and sighs. 'Oh, maybe it's just a scar from you picking at your face.'

'I don't pick—'

Mum cuts me off. 'Your father has been a nightmare today.'

I stop myself rolling my eyes (because I know Mum will start shrieking about wrinkles) and suppress a sigh.

'Why? What's he done?'

'I bloody asked him to sort out the curtains in the living room. People were meant to come today to hang them up – but did they arrive? No! Did he sort it out? No! He should bloody well put his money where his mouth is. How am I meant to have my girls over when the living room looks so cheap?'

I mumble something in reply and, after a couple of minutes of listening to Mum complain, manage to slip out by saying I've got homework to do.

As I go up the stairs, I catch sight of myself in the floor-length hall mirror (our house is literally covered in mirrors. I counted them once: twenty-two) and am struck by how different I look at home versus school or out. My shoulders are hunched, my eyes are downcast. It's like without other people, I just wither away. I hate being by myself, being at home. I need my friends to bring me to life.

When I get to my room, I peel off my school clothes and hang them up in my wardrobe. Sitting on my bed, I open

YouTube and start watching the best ways to stop under-eye concealer creasing.

As I'm watching, my phone lights up. For a split second, my heart leaps – could it be Tom?

But it's not. It's just some random creepy guy commenting on my Instagram again.

I don't even open the app. I just tap straight through to mine and Tom's old WhatsApp thread.

The last messages from him are angry, and they immediately make me frown, but I don't want to see those. I tap search and try a few phrases, looking for the very first messages sent between us from around six months ago, when we first started dating. It takes me almost five minutes of searching the chat to find them, but eventually I do.

I scroll through, remembering how much I agonized over every text. The excitement I felt when I read his sweet words for the first time. I reread the first few, one at a time, then skip to the messages after our first kiss, and the first time he said I looked beautiful.

Tears spill down my cheeks.

It wasn't my fault. It was him. Not me. Him.

That's what everyone said. *That's right, isn't it?*

I sniff, scrolling all the way down to our final messages. The pain almost radiates out from the screen. Once again, I think back to his hardened face when I told him it was over.

I did the right thing.

*Did I do the right thing?*

I catch sight of myself in my table mirror. Black tears have melted my make-up over half my face. I know I look disgusting.

There's not a person alive who would say I look attractive right now.

My phone buzzes again angrily. I swipe the message open.

> **Sven_247** You've probably got way better things to do right now, but fancy a WhatsApp call?

I stare at his profile icon. He's bent over, tensing, and you can see the dark outline of his biceps.

He's a massive try-hard, obviously. He's also not Tom.

But I need to be brought back to life again – I need to stop feeling like *this*. I dab my eyes with my fingertips and start typing.

> **Chlo03** Sure, why not.

# CHAPTER 5

## *Amber*

It's Saturday afternoon, and while everyone else my age is either out with their friends or having a lie-in, my parents are forcing me to go round a garden centre with them.

This morning, Mum started becoming obsessed with taking me out somewhere. Seb is staying away all weekend at a football training session and match with his local club, and when he left to get the minibus, Mum just kept watching me sitting on the sofa refreshing my phone screen, until eventually she yanked on my arm and said, 'Right! We're all going out.'

Of course, I didn't want to go anywhere. Actually, the last thing I want to be doing on a Saturday is traipsing around a garden centre with my parents, but I didn't want to make her upset, so here I am, skimming through plants with big, waxy leaves that droop almost to the floor.

It's not like Dad wants to be here either. Right now, he's walking along next to me, hands in his pockets, shoulders slumped, head down. In fact, if he wasn't a fifty-year-old man and I wasn't a sixteen-year-old girl, we'd probably look more like twins than me and Seb.

Dad sees me glancing at him and gives me a small smile. I smile back before looking away.

Mum is out in front, whizzing around, her dark hair flicking from side to side as she holds up pots and plants, shouting at both of us.

'Robert! Amber! What do you think?'

She's balancing the plants on either side of her hips with a quizzical expression, biting one side of her lip.

'Would this suit the front room? Or would this?'

She's talking so fast that I don't catch most of what she's saying, and from Dad's blank expression, I don't think he did either.

'You two! Come over here! I want to show you . . .'

As Mum keeps talking, I mutter something about wanting to look at some plants for my bedroom and then slink off in the opposite direction.

Walking around the corner of the shop, I find myself standing next to a selection of tiny painted ceramic pots with spiky cactuses and shiny-leaved plants. They look cool. I can almost picture buying these myself. Not being here with my parents, but maybe being with Ren, searching the shelves, choosing our favourites to decorate our new flat.

Maybe we'd argue. Or he'd laugh at me as I picked up that strange little pot painted with cat faces, insisting that we buy it.

Then later, once our tiny home was filled with plants, we'd cosy up on the sofa together and put on the TV. Maybe he'd put his arm around me, lean down to kiss me. Maybe we'd forget about the TV show altogether . . .

I'm so deep in thought that it takes me a few seconds to realize that the person directly in front of me is wearing a royal-blue personal  trainer T-shirt striped with orange.

My stomach tightens.

'Oh, hey again!'

I nearly jump out of my skin at the sound of Iulia's voice. She's reaching for one of the tools on the top shelf and smiles at me.

My mouth hangs open for a few seconds. I don't know what exactly I'm supposed to say. Hello back? It's too late for that, surely.

Oh God, why aren't I saying anything?

*Say something!*

Iulia has turned back again, placing one foot on the bottom shelf so she can reach the gardening fork.

'ThanksforyourhelpinthegymonWednesday,' I blurt out so quickly that it sounds like one syllable.

Iulia turns back to me, frowning. 'Sorry?' she says, 'Oh yeah! No worries.'

'I mean, it was all my fault. I'm so bad at exercise.'

Iulia hops down from the shelves deftly and then looks at me, her head on one side. 'What kinda exercise do you want to get into?'

My cheeks start heating up. 'Oh, I don't know, really . . . I don't . . .'

'Have you tried high-intensity interval training?' Iulia's eyes light up, and she suddenly starts talking about these different workouts she does each day.

'Look – I've got a clip.' She passes me her phone, already open on a video where several people are frantically pulling themselves up with their arms.

23

There's no way I could ever, *ever* do that.

Iulia looks like she's waiting for a response. I don't know quite what to say to her, so I just stare fixedly at the screen.

There's a crash from somewhere nearby. Iulia's eyes fly open. 'Oh crap! That's probably my niece. I'm meant to be watching her. Just a sec!'

In lightning speed, she's dashed off round the corner, and I'm left staring at her unlocked phone.

A creeping thought comes over me.

This is Iulia's phone. With all Iulia's contacts in it.

And she works with Ren at the gym; she sees him every day.

You usually have the number of the people you work with, don't you? Particularly if you are on the same training course *and* go to college together.

If I can get Ren's number, I'll be able to see when he's online on WhatsApp. I'll be able to add his Snapchat. Maybe I can find out a bit more about why he's in trouble at the gym . . .

My pulse is speeding up.

*Am I actually going to do this?*

Without thinking too much about what my fingers are doing, I tap out of the short video on Iulia's phone and pull up the home screen. With shaking hands, I quickly type *Ren Moore* into her contact list. His number comes up instantly – the top result.

Looking around, I pull out my own phone and take a photo of the contact number.

Iulia comes round the corner just as I tap back on the video.

# CHAPTER 6

## Chloe

The soft pink duvet is crumpled like creased paper around me. I grab a handful of the covers and pull them over my mouth as I splutter with laughter.

It's 2 a.m., and I mustn't wake Mum or Dad, who are sleeping silently two rooms along.

I feel my cheeks burning from smiling so much as I press my phone to my ear.

'Stop it!' I hiss. But I can't hang up. It's like we're tethered by some strange power. It's almost like this isn't the first time we've spoken.

'*Are you always this giggly?*' says Sven, his voice deep and gravelly down the line.

I try to stop the grin from being obvious in my voice. 'Are you always this rude?'

Sven's voice cracks. '*Me?!*'

I giggle and dive once more under the covers.

'*Right. I'm offended! Goodbye!*' he says.

'OK. Goodbye. I mean . . . you're not the only guy to call me.'

'*You're not the only girl to call me*,' he quips back.

There's a soft thump from the other room, and I glance at the clock.

I really should hang up and go to sleep for school in a few hours. I don't even know this guy. But there's something about the way he speaks to me. When we first chatted, his voice was quiet, and I could tell he was nervous. And then when he later admitted he was 'pretty shocked' I agreed to call him considering how I looked in my Instagram, it was like I was some kind of unattainable goddess. Like he thought I was pretty.

He's only seen the photos of me online, with my stomach sucked in, waist twisted to the side so my back curves in sharply.

Seeing myself through his eyes makes a weird tingling feeling sweep up my neck and across my cheeks.

If I say goodbye and go to sleep, I have to lie here by myself. I have to think about school tomorrow, sitting with Tom on the field. Pretend that every imperfection on my face, every spidery eyelash or crust of concealer, doesn't scream at me whenever he looks my way.

Here, lying on my bed in the dark with no make-up on, speaking to Sven . . . I feel like me.

Almost on cue, he starts speaking again. His voice isn't teasing, but soft.

'*When I rang you tonight, I never thought you would still be speaking to me at 2 a.m.*'

The hairs on the back of my arm prickle.

'It's a shame you're not around, y'know,' I say, softer too.

Sven lowers his voice to almost a whisper. '*I'd love to be there.*'

Something makes a lump form in my throat. I'm already thinking of the last time I spoke to someone like this. When me and Tom were lying together on his bed, and he gently brushed an eyelash off my cheek, before kissing my eyelid.

Nibbling my lip, I drag one of my sharp nails across the back of my arm, which causes a blotchy red line.

'I-I should go.'

Sven sucks in his breath. '*Sorry. Th-that was too much. I shouldn't have—*'

'Nah, it's cool,' I say, but something is bothering me.

We've never even met each other. Why is this guy apologizing for being 'too much'? I've been talking to him all night – and why? For all I know, he could be some complete weirdo. I need to stop this.

Sven's deep voice cuts through my thoughts. '*Everything just feels so natural with you, I can't help it. I know I'd be tongue-tied if I ever saw someone as beautiful as you in person.*'

I try to keep frowning, but I can't.

'Oh, shut up,' I say.

It honestly takes about ten more minutes for us to hang up the phone.

As I lie on the back of the bed, I start scrolling through Sven's Instagram feed. His muscles burst out from every photo. His jet-black hair casts a shadow across his sharp cheekbones.

I mean, he's definitely attractive. Definitely better looking than Tom. Tom is a bit lanky, if you really look at him. He's tall, yes – like six foot four – but almost too tall. He's got a

27

skinny chest, and because he always towers above everyone, he kind of hunches down, which makes his limbs look even more gangly.

So why do I feel a weird tug in my chest when I see him?

Ugh. Look – he's not thinking about me. I need to get a grip. It's over.

I click through to the Facebook invite page for Tom's party. Rachel, Louise, Ameerah – everyone we hang out with from school is on the invite list.

What if Tom gets with someone at the party? What if he completely blanks me?

I think of our final argument, when black mascara tears were streaming down my face. I can't let that be how he remembers me.

Climbing out of bed, I tiptoe across the room to my wardrobe and start pulling out dresses. I pick out the green sequinned dress again and run my fingers across the feathered hem.

I try to think how Tom is going to react when he sees me in it. Whether he'll try to speak to me. Or whether I'll chat to the other guys, and he'll watch me. I don't even really know what I want to happen. I just want him to see me.

When I slip back into bed, my vision is blurring. Shaking my head, I pull the warm duvet up high to my neck.

I start clicking through Tom's Instagram pictures, all of which I've seen a million times.

A tear dribbles down my nose.

My phone dings with a DM. It's Sven.

**Sven_247** Can't stop thinking about you.

28

My eyes are heavy as my finger hovers over the message, not quite sure whether to open it. After a few seconds, I tap the screen on lock and drop the phone onto the bed.

Closing my eyes, I think of Sven lying in his own bed, flicking through my photos, and thinking of me.

# CHAPTER 7

## Amber

My ears, nose and cheeks are turning pink from the chill in the wind as I walk home after school on Monday night. For the last week, my thoughts have been stuck on Ren Moore and what those two receptionists said: '*That manager always had it in for him.*' I can imagine what she's like – always sneering when he's a minute late and finding any excuse to get him in trouble.

I spent the whole of last weekend refreshing Ren's Instagram, Twitter and the public profile of his Facebook page, trying to work out if I can glean what's really going on.

I'm not paying attention to my feet – I just keep refreshing his profiles, clicking through to a couple of his friend's Instagrams to see if there are any new photos of him I may have missed.

I bite at a hangnail on my thumb as I exit the app and open Snapchat.

After I came back from the garden centre on Saturday, I set up a fake profile and added Ren on Snapchat. He almost instantly accepted, but so far he hasn't posted anything.

Part of me wants to delete him from my friends list. What if we do actually speak, and he sees I've set up a fake account so I can see his Snapchats? What if he ever found out how I got his number?

My hand hovers over the gear icon. I know I should delete him. It's too weird, too risky. I shouldn't be looking at his Snapchats under a fake name.

But . . . what if it gives me a clue about what's going on?

Plus, he accepted the friend request of someone he doesn't know. He can't mind about privacy that much. It's not like I forced him to add me as a friend.

I'm tapping at the screen when I accidentally swipe something, and my phone changes.

## Welcome to Snap
## Map!

_____

## Location access is required to use the
## Map.

I blink.

Does this . . . actually *work*?

Within a few seconds, I've tapped through to the map. There's a dark-haired male avatar several streets away. When I click on the avatar, I can clearly see the name *Ren Moore*.

My feet stop moving.

He's two streets away from me. Just two streets.

Shaking my head, I lock my phone screen. I should ignore this. I should keep walking and go straight home.

So what if he's sharing his location? He clearly doesn't mean for *me* to see it. With my fake name, he doesn't even know I have him on Snap Map.

The Snapchat ghost winks at me. But still, he's so close, just a few streets away. I don't have to say anything – I can just wander by, see what he's up to. It might help me find out what's going on with his manager.

My mind doesn't make a decision; my feet do. They've already starting walking in the opposite direction, turning down a side street, tracing the route towards Ren's location.

The blood starts to drum in my head.

I *really* shouldn't be doing this.

But Ren hasn't been at the gym in the past week. Something must be going on. I want to help him.

But it's not just that, is it . . . ?

If I'm completely honest, part of me just wants to see him again. I want to talk to him, and I want him to know that whatever his manager has said, I'm on his side.

My breath is coming in short bursts, and I realize I've broken into a run.

I'm getting closer to his location avatar. My heart is speeding up. It feels like something is going to happen. He's going to remember me – and smile. His beautiful speckled grey eyes . . . His strong arms.

My location dot is almost directly on top of his avatar. I look up and find I'm standing directly in front of a semi-detached house. There's a light on in the second-floor front window, and through the blinds, I can just about make out a dark figure crouched over a computer screen.

I squint, trying to see more clearly. Suddenly the figure moves towards the window, and I almost jump out of my skin. Without looking back, I bolt away from the house, my entire body trembling from head to toe.

While I run, I keep shaking my head, trying to clear my thoughts. But I can't stop them – they're coming in thick and fast, breaking through the cracks.

Why the hell did I just turn up at someone's house?

There is something *seriously* wrong with me.

Tears start streaming down my face. I run the whole way home, not stopping to catch a breath, hating every single inch of myself.

# CHAPTER 8

# Chloe

Thursday night, I'm in my bedroom, looking in the mirror at the green sequinned material stretched across my hips. There's plucks of feathers along the short hem tickling my thighs, and the sequins mean my chest glimmers as I move.

It's too much, isn't it?

I'm wearing my favourite push-up bra, so my breasts are spilling out of the top, and I didn't actually realize how tight the stretchy fabric would be across the top of my thighs. I don't want to look like I'm wearing a second skin, like my mum!

I've lined my eyes in dark kohl along the upper lashes and stuck individual false lashes on the outer corners. I've painted my lips dark red to compliment the depth of the sea-green dress.

I smooth the thin material taut against my stomach.

Tonight will be fine. Tom will see me looking like this, and hopefully he'll stare. I can flirt with guys. I can just have a good time and ignore him.

My phone vibrates with a message.

> **Sven_247** WOW

I grin and pull my phone towards me. Earlier, I sent him a selfie of what I'm wearing to the party.

> **Sven_247** You look unbelievable. Can't believe I'm not there to see you like that in person.

I send an embarrassed-face emoji by way of response and slip my phone into my pocket. We've been messaging almost non-stop since that phone call, and he's asked me if I want to call again tonight, after the party.

It feels almost like I have my own secret person tucked away in my pocket. Any time I feel a pang about Tom or stress out about Mum, I can just get out my phone and start messaging him.

Maybe it's not normal to do that to someone you don't know. But we've chatted on the phone. I know his voice. I feel like I actually do know him.

Without paying attention to what my hands are doing, I click open Tom's Instagram page. He's put up a photo of seven crates of beer they've bought with the caption *Just a quiet one tonight.*

There's a weird feeling at the bottom of my stomach. To be honest, part of me doesn't want to go. I want to crawl back into bed and start messaging Sven, call him again and stay up all night giggling – not to have to face Tom.

Staring at myself in the mirror, I slowly twist my red lipstick back into its case. As I flick my hair over my shoulder, there's a soapy smell of leave-in conditioner.

I suck my breath in. Right. Time to go.

*** 

Andy, one of Tom's friend's from Year Twelve, is looking down at me, clutching a beer. It's warm, too warm, in Tom's living room, and as his parents are away, the entire house is thumping with music. I glance around, but the edge of the room is getting fuzzy. I stare at Andy's lips, try to focus on what he's saying back to me, but to be honest, I'm not paying attention.

Glancing sideways, I surreptitiously scan the room. Tom is in the far corner, lugging a cart of beers across the hall, and our eyes meet for a split second. I clutch Andy's arm and laugh, hard, at what he just said – pressing my boobs against his chest.

I glance back at Tom, but he's already gone.

Andy follows my gaze, then clears his throat.

'I've – er, got to go and get a beer,' he says, turning away.

There's another group of guys that quickly arrive though, and I jump straight into the centre – laughing, chatting and giggling.

Within seconds, they are teasing me, trying to catch my attention. I feel like I'm slipping back into my own skin as I start talking loudly. It's easy; it doesn't even take work.

Tom has moved to the outer corner of the group. He keeps

flicking his hair to one side, like he always does when he's agitated.

The more people crowd around me, the more he flicks. A warm glow rises up my chest as I notice him staring at me.

I shout out a joke, louder than everyone else in the room – which causes almost all the guys to laugh.

At that moment, Tom comes over, his face set.

He looks straight at me. I can tell he's had a drink – he's got that one-eye-half-closed expression he gets when his brain has turned to treacle.

Tom looks like he's about to speak to me, so I turn to face him . . . but instead, he suddenly swivels round – his back against me – shutting me out of the group.

Anger rises up in my chest. Without thinking about what I'm doing, I cut across Tom to Seb and lightly touch his arm.

'Can't believe you downed that beer so quickly,' I say with a giggle.

Seb's eyes light up, and he turns to face me fully. Out of the corner of my eye, I see Tom's face, his eyes dark.

I smile and keep chatting, one hand resting on my chest. When I look up, Tom has left. Not just our conversation, the entire room.

*Shit.* Where's he gone?

Seb leans in and puts a hand on my waist. Smiling, I gently move his hand away.

'Excuse me, I've just got to go and, um, find someone.'

I pick my way through the crowd. Several people shout my name to get me to come over, but I shake my head, smiling.

It's all so familiar, this bloody house. Every room reminds me of him.

My head is thumping now. Painful. I wince and pick my legs up across each step of the stairs. I don't even think about where I'm going. Right to the end of the corridor. Tom's bedroom.

When I push open the door, there's Louise and Jerome entangled on the bedsheets. They haven't seen me. With a half-smile, I slowly click the door shut. Hmm. Will have to ask her about that later.

With a sigh, I open the door to Tom's little brother's room and go to sit down on the bed.

It's dark – and when I focus, I see a dark, lanky figure hunched over the bed.

I nearly leap out of my skin.

Tom looks up. He's swigging a beer, which is obscuring his face – but even in the dim light, I can tell it's him by the way he moves. I sit down next to him. He narrows his gaze.

'You should go and join the party,' he says gruffly.

I lean in and nudge my forehead against his shoulder.

He breathes out slowly. 'No, really. You should go and join the party.'

'I just want to stay here with you,' I say, looking up at him. And all of a sudden, I don't want to be loud and obnoxious. I just want to sit here, with Tom, and cry.

Tom doesn't react.

'We really need to talk, T,' I say.

Tom stands up, yanking my head off his shoulder. He stands over me, gritting his teeth.

'What the bloody hell are you doing at my party, anyway, Chloe?!'

# CHAPTER 9

## Chloe

Tom is staring down at me, his face like thunder.

'What do you mean?' I say. 'I'm just at your party like everyone else.'

He looks like he wants to say something else, but he doesn't. Instead, he rakes his hands through his hair and looks away.

'You know exactly what you're doing.'

There's a twist in my stomach, like it's all my fault. But . . . I didn't . . .

Tom's face is pained, and suddenly I want to throw my arms around him.

'I'm—' I stutter. 'I didn't mean—'

Tom looks down at the bed and sighs. 'Yes, you did. You always know what you're doing. You always mean to do it.'

I feel a flash of anger. 'That's unfair. You weren't even interested in me!'

'Christ. Not this again.'

'Guys message me all the time, you know. They actually want to speak to me.'

Tom looks up. 'So do I.'

'Yeah, sure. That's why you were texting Samantha – that's why Kaylie kept sending you all those Snapchats.'

He stares at me – this six-foot-four man with stubble across his cheeks – and his eyes widen like a child's.

'I didn't ask her to ! She sent them to everyone. For God's sake, Chloe.' Tom's lower lip is sticking out. 'Why do you flirt like that with everyone? Why do you do that to me?'

I nibble my lip, but then shake my head. 'Why shouldn't I act how I like? We're not together – not any more.'

The edge of Tom's jaw catches the low light as it clenches in the darkness. 'I know. You made that clear.'

Instinctively I reach my hand out towards his, but in one fluid motion, he draws himself up to his full height and walks out of the room. I blink at the spot where he stood.

Part of me wants to scream at him to come back. But another part wants to walk out, pretend he's not here, and go straight into the arms of another guy.

*I. Don't. Need. Him.*

I look down at my phone. Shit – the battery's dead.

The sheets on the bed are lightly rumpled where Tom was sitting. I glance at it for a moment.

*Screw him.*

Seriously. He was the one who didn't care, messaging all those other girls. Now he tries to pretend that he still wants us to be together?

I tap my phone again to message Sven, but the screen stays resolutely black. Huh.

I stand up.

Oh *God*. I shouldn't have done that so quickly. The room is swaying in front of me – the colours in the dim light blurring into one. I step forward and flick on the light switch, but it's worse, horrifically bright.

I stand there for a moment – not sure what to do. But then I catch sight of myself in the mirror. My eyeliner is slightly smudged, and my red lipstick has faded to a pale pink – but I'm surprised by how pretty I look compared to my normal, bare face.

Most of my make-up is just how I applied it, and the green sequinned dress matches perfectly with my dark glossy hair. I square my shoulders.

I'm not going to let Tom get to me.

I'm going back out there.

\*\*\*

Half an hour later, I'm draped on the armrest of a sofa, staring into the eyes of this guy, Joshua. At least I think he's called J-something. He's from Andy's football team, or rugby team . . . maybe.

Anyway, I like talking to him.

He's almost good-looking – far-apart eyes, strong nose – and he's fun to speak to, kinda.

Tom is nowhere to be seen, but I don't care. I look right into whatshisname's eyes, his pupils widen, and I giggle at something he says. As I lean closer, I notice his nose is slightly too upturned. But he's tall, with strong shoulders. He definitely works out – his muscles are bulging out of his tight T-shirt.

I grin, and – so fast the room goes out of focus – he leans forward and clashes his lips against mine.

There's an urgency in his hot, wet mouth, forcing his face against mine. His big hand clumsily snakes down my back and rests on my bum. For some reason, I suddenly feel sick.

I pull away sharply, opening my eyes. The lights are bright. Too bright.

'I feel a bit . . . I don't know.' I clutch my head, my vision swimming. 'I said I'd be home. I need to head back.'

At once, J-something has leaped up and taken my arm.

'Yeah, sure,' he says, smiling. 'I'll walk you back.'

'No – it's . . . I'm fine,' I say, but as I try to walk, I stumble. The guy laughs and puts his hand on my waist.

'You can barely stand.' He grins. 'C'mon – you need help.'

I let him lead me out of the party. My mind is foggy, but somewhere beyond the mist, a little voice is telling me to get away. I take his arm off of my waist, peel his hand off of my bum – but then I sway straight into him. He laughs and puts his hands back to steady me.

'What are you like,' he says, standing too close to me as he manoeuvres me along the pavement, his eyes travelling down my body.

As we get closer to my house, I turn to him.

'I know my way back from here – it's OK. I can get home now,' I say.

There's a pause.

'Thanks,' I mutter, trying to keep my words straight, but they feel too big for my mouth.

He scoffs. 'Don't be ridiculous. What sort of a guy would I be if I let you walk home by yourself in this state?'

There's something determined about his voice that makes the skin on the back of my arms tighten.

'It's fine, honestly,' I say.

He shakes his head, running his hand up my waist, higher so he's touching the edge of my bra strap over the top of my dress.

There's a horrible tight feeling in my stomach.

*Why won't he leave?*

I smile, putting on a light, non-drunk voice. 'Seriously, I'm fine!'

Even though it makes my stomach feel even sicker, I touch his chest, trying to sound calm.

J-something grins. 'Aw, OK,  then.'

My whole body relaxes.

*Thank God.*

'. . . but not without a goodbye kiss.'

I dutifully lift my chin up, relieved that this will soon be over, but he shakes his head.

'No, over there.'

He indicates towards a row of trees down an alcove between the houses.

'It's quieter,' he says.

'No. I . . . I don't want—'

But he's not listening. He pulls me along, and in what seems like a matter of seconds he's pressed me up against one of the trees and his warm mouth is moving against mine. His lips are too wet and puffy. I can feel my body tense up, trying to squirm away from him – but he responds by gripping my head.

'You're a wriggler, aren't you,' he says with a smirk, clashing his mouth against my teeth.

'I . . .' I try to say something, but I can't – his lips are suffocating me.

He presses his large, hard body against mine, and I'm pinned to the tree. He breaks away from me and starts moving his thick hands over my breasts. He squeezes them so hard it's painful.

'No. I'm not . . . I don't—' I start breathlessly, but my voice is too quiet.

He presses his lips against my neck, and through the fog I feel a tear run down my cheek.

It takes every effort of my trembling limbs to lift up my hands and push him away, hard. His body rocks back in shock.

And then through the thick darkness, I run and run and run.

# CHAPTER 10

# Amber

On Friday morning, as soon as the bell goes for break, I walk as fast as I can towards the back of the school to nab the single bench that faces the PE changing rooms.

This is my usual spot. There's no one else around, and I'm relieved to find it empty. As I sit down, I suppress a shiver and clutch my hands together. The wind circles my bare ankles and there are tiny flecks of dry skin, which are starting to crack around my knuckles.

Oh God – *why* did I turn up at Ren's house last night?

I bet that was him in the second-floor room. He probably spotted me out of the window before I ran away. Do you think he could see my face?

I dig my nails into my palm so hard that they hurt.

Ren probably thinks I'm some kind of stalker now. I bet he point-blank ignores me next time I step foot in the gym. That's if I can ever bear to again.

*Oh God.*

I clutch my head in my hands. I'm trying to stop the thoughts from going round and round my brain, but I can't. They're stuck on a stupid, predictable loop. There isn't a mute switch. I can't turn it off.

Ren's probably laughing at me right now. Looking at my Instagram with no photos on it, thinking I'm this pathetic high school girl who waits for him outside his house.

The darkness created by my palms is soothing, kinda.

There's a muffled sound of a familiar, distant voice.

I lift my head out of my hands, squinting, to see who's speaking. A strand of hair flops out of my bun and over my face.

Seb is walking over in the direction of the concourse with a huge gang of guys from our year. He's staring at me and has a slight frown.

'Sis!' he shouts, seemingly oblivious to the attention he's drawing.

The guys around him glance at me. Oh, why can't he ever be quiet? My cheeks start to heat up.

'What you doing? You all right?' he hollers.

I pull a face at him and nod by way of response – desperate to make him stop talking.

'*Fine*,' I mouth.

Seb stops walking – he looks dangerously close to coming over.

I clear my throat. 'I'm just reading. *R-e-a-d-i-n-g*.' I mouth the letters, pulling out my phone and gesticulating towards the screen.

Everyone is looking at me. A hotness sweeps up my neck and across my cheeks. I stare at Seb, trying to laserbeam my thoughts into his brain: *Please stop talking*.

Seb's eyes snap with recognition, and then he smiles, waving at me as he wanders off with his group.

I unlock my phone and start actually reading, the heat in my face simmering down.

It's open on Ren's Instagram page. There's hundreds of photos of him, all of which I've already seen. I start clicking through the images, back further and further, until I find ones he's tagged in from when he was in Year Seven.

He looks so tiny, like a little child. His cheeks big and round, skin tanned, and hair a messy mop of black.

My heart starts to ache. I really can't believe he's having such a tough time with his manager. He's so lovely. It's bullying, really.

I look down at my cracked hands. I can't let my stupid nerves get in the way of helping. After all, Ren would do the same for me. Like when I first went to the gym: he came over, asked me what body area I wanted to work on, and drew me up an entire workout plan without me even asking. He was clearly busy – people kept coming to ask him for advice – but he stayed and talked me through all of it.

Getting up off my bench, I start walking towards the leisure centre, which is attached to the school PE block. I ignore the crowds of people standing and nattering. Usually I would feel embarrassed walking by myself – but today I have a purpose.

When I get to the entrance, I walk straight up to the woman on the front desk.

She's standing behind the counter, leaning to one side, raking a long-fingernailed hand through one of her blonde curls.

I clear my throat.

'Can I help you?' she says, only half looking at me.

I swallow. 'Is Ren Moore here?'

49

'No, I'm afraid he no longer works here.'

*Wait – what?*

'What – why did he leave?' I blurt out.

The woman looks at me fully – my too-big jumper, my greasy skin – then shakes her head. 'I'm afraid I can't tell you that information. It's confidential.'

Oh God. What have I said? I sound and look like such a freak. But it's about to get worse. It's like my tongue doesn't connect with my brain. My lips are shaking, but they still keep moving.

'But I have to know. I really have to know. I'm . . .'

I inhale.

'. . . his sister.'

The receptionist's eyes widen.

'You're his sister?'

'Yes.' My cheeks are burning so much, I feel like they might actually catch alight.

She purses her lips.

'Just a moment. I need to speak to someone. Wait here.'

# CHAPTER 11

## *Chloe*

The next morning, my head is thumping so hard I can't move.

Lying face down on my duvet, I feel numb.

Completely and utterly numb. Like someone has plunged me into a bucket of ice. I try to nudge my arm up from underneath my chest, but I can't.

My breath is coming in short, sharp bursts.

I don't want to think about last night, but the feeling of that guy pressing me against the tree keeps coming back to me. His hands running up and down my body. His big face forcing itself onto mine. At one point, I thought he wasn't going to stop. I've never felt scared like that with a guy before. Thank God I managed to push him off and get away.

*Oh God.* I think I'm going to be sick!

I leap up and run to the bathroom, feeling like death. I kneel on the cold tiled floor and dry-heave into the bowl.

I stare into the toilet, retching, tears running down my cheeks.

There's a shrill voice from the other side of the door.

'Oh, for God's sake. I need to use the bathroom. Look at you – hungover, and school today as well!'

I clutch my ears to blot out Mum's screechy voice, and retch again.

There's a long, drawn-out sigh from the other side of the bathroom door, then I hear her padding off to her en suite.

I push out my hands in front of me. The tendons are shaking so hard they look like they might snap.

\*\*\*

Twenty minutes later, I manage to stumble back to bed. I pull the duvet high up over me – catching sight of lipstick stains across the bedspread which I'll have to wash before Mum sees and freaks out.

I sigh and plug in the charger on my phone. The time flashes up – thirty minutes until I have to make it into school.

I need to tell someone.

*Louise?*

For a brief moment I consider it, but something makes me pause. I can imagine her face when she hears what happened, her eyes alight in a mixture of sympathy and delight.

I shake my head. No – she's my friend. She would care.

But I still don't call her.

*Tom?*

My ears start to prickle at the thought. He knew I walked off with . . . What even was his name – Joshua? John??

Even if he didn't see, he'll have heard about it. He will hate my guts.

The first contact that appears when my phone loads up is Sven. There's a flurry of messages.

> **Sven_247** Hey, gorgeous. How are you? How's your night going?

> **Sven_247** Just looked back at your Instagram pic. Wow.

> **Sven_247** How's the party going?

> **Sven_247** What's up?

> **Sven_247** What is going on?! Why aren't you replying?

There's something about seeing five messages in a row that makes my stomach feel even queasier.

God, what is wrong with me today? It's fine. He always texts loads; it's just because he cares.

And right now I need someone who cares more than anything.

I click open the phone and type a message.

**Chlo03** Sorry! My phone died. Had a bit of a night.

The phone lights up with his online symbol almost instantly. Then I see *Sven is typing* . . .

I wonder how he replies so quickly. Does he sit around all day, waiting for my messages? I push the thought to the back of my mind. I need someone like that. He's so different to anyone else – Mum, or Tom. He's completely focused on me. And it's nice.

**Sven_247** Nah, it's cool. I just got worried about you when you didn't reply. How was your night?

My stomach turns over as I dredge up the memory. His hands over me, his face on mine. Thankfully I got away after that, but not before he had almost grabbed my breast out of my dress.

I blink at the screen and start typing.

Somehow, everything comes out. What J did. Tom. What happened at the party. I type and type and type. Like it's not Sven, but a diary. Somehow it feels so much easier to tell this to Sven than it does to tell my mum. Or Tom. Or Louise. Or anyone. I can just type the words and get it all off my chest. And I know he'll understand.

There's a pause after I hit send. I can see Sven is still online, but for the first time he doesn't start typing immediately.

I reread my words, splayed out across the screen. And a pric
kling sensation runs across my arms.

My eyes widen.

*Shit. What have I done?*

I don't even know this guy. He could just ignore me right
now, and I would look like a complete idiot.

His icon lights up with the words, *Sven is typing . . .* and relief
floods through my veins.

What is wrong with me at the moment? My thoughts are so
hysterical. Maybe I'll ignore his next message. Take a couple of
hours to reply to him. Yes, that'll do it. That'll make me feel OK
again.

My phone dings.

I frown at the screen.

What the—

> **Sven_247** You got with a guy?

> **Sven_247** ??

> **Sven_247** What did you expect?

I stare down at the phone, bile rising in my throat. It's dinging
every few seconds. Sven is sending a question mark in each new
message.

I throw my phone under the duvet, but it keeps dinging. Every sound makes my teeth stand on edge.

I blink at my shaking hands.

*What did you expect?*

I glance at my short sequinned green dress, crumpled beneath me on the floor, and my phone vibrates again.

**Sven_247** Slut.

I think of me looking at Tom on the other side of the room, flirting with all those guys. I feel hot humiliation course through my body. I clasp my hands to my chest.

Rocking back and forth, I can feel J's hands running over my breasts. I take a ragged breath, open my mouth, and howl silently so Mum can't hear – black tears streaking down my cheeks.

But I can't make it stop. I can't take it back.

Under the covers, the phone keeps buzzing.

*DingDingDingDingDing.*

# CHAPTER 12

## *Amber*

The manager of the leisure centre leans across her desk. Her shoulders are broad, and she takes up most of the bare wood as she rests her muscular arms on the tabletop. We're in a tiny room without windows, just to the right of the main gym area, and the electric lighting is making it feel like an interrogation.

My mouth turns dry.

The manager has her head tilted to one side, lips pursed, and her small eyes open wide. She speaks now in a deep, soft tone. I can barely look at her. I twist my fingers round and round in my palm and notice another speck of blood on my dry skin.

I only catch snatches of what she's saying.

'. . . sorry. I can't divulge this information, even to his sister . . . Suffice to say there were several incidents, and Ren has now left this employment.'

*Incidents?*

I really can't imagine Ren being involved in any k ind of 'incident', it just doesn't seem right.

My heart aches as I think of him sitting at home, staring at the computer, alone, depressed. It's so incredibly unfair.

'H-he wasn't involved,' I blurt out before I can stop myself.

The manager blinks. 'Excuse me?'

My cheeks flush. 'Sorry . . . um – he wasn't involved in the incidents.'

'Who wasn't?'

'Ren. He can't have been. I know, um, him.' The woman is staring at me like I've grown an extra head. I take a deep breath. 'I think . . . he's innocent.'

The manager closes her mouth and gives a deep sigh. 'Amber . . . Moore – is it?'

'Yes,' I whisper.

'Well, Amber, I can't go into details, but I can assure you the decision to let Ren go wasn't taken lightly.'

'What – you mean *you* fired him?' I say, my voice sharper than I was intending.

At that moment, the bell rings distantly, signalling the end of break. The manager glances at the school crest on my jumper. She stands up.

'I'm sorry, that's all we have time for. Would you like me to speak to your teachers, let them know what we've been talking about? I'm sure they'd be happy to offer you some support.'

'No!' I stand up so fast my backpack bumps the back of the chair I've been sitting on. 'I mean, no – um, I'm fine.'

'OK – well if you have any more co—'

But I don't hear the end of her sentence. I've already pushed open the door and am walking back through the corridor, out of the leisure centre.

I walk so fast I start to get out of breath. Across the empty playground, through the concourse, towards the humanities block.

As my pulse speeds up, my thoughts do too. I can imagine Ren's face when he was told he was fired.

'*Incidents.*'

I see his sweet face crumpling when he was fired. I think of him, again, smiling at me, putting his hand on my shoulder.

He barely knows me, really, but he still made the time to help me.

It's just so unfair. And wrong.

As I'm walking to class, I'm so engrossed in my thoughts I don't recognize a familiar deep, throaty laugh and a high, tinkling one until I'm right next to them both.

I blink.

Seb and Chloe are at the end of the corridor. She has her hand on her hip and her glossy hair flicked over one shoulder.

Seb is leaning forward, gesticulating wildly as he talks and grinning at her. His eyes are fixed on Chloe so much he doesn't even notice me.

Seb hops between his two feet before shouting something and heading to class. Chloe smiles at him, shaking her head, and then steps into the classroom. She glances at me, and I feel myself flush a deep scarlet.

Oh, God – did she see me staring?

With my eyes fixed on the ground, I follow them in and sit down. I swear I almost saw a flash of disgust in Chloe's eye. She probably no longer wants to speak to Seb just because she knows he's my twin.

And Ren – who am I kidding? Even if I help him get rehired,

he'll never like me. Why would he? He's so good- looking, he could have literally anyone he wanted.

I put my head down flat on the desk and stay like that for the rest of the lesson.

# CHAPTER 13

## Chloe

Seb is standing outside class, leaning towards me. He's smiling, but his expression seems strained.

'Yeah, good night,' he says, 'but when I was heading back about midnight, I could've sworn I saw something. You and that guy from footy – What's his name? James? – by the trees.' Seb runs one hand across the back of his neck, his eyes focused on the wall behind me. 'It didn't look right. Was he . . . Were you OK?'

For a split second my eyes widen, but then I quickly rearrange my features and roll my eyes. 'Yeah.' I snort. 'Why wouldn't I be OK?'

In the classroom behind us, one of the guys shouts a joke and Seb shouts back. Before he has a chance to say any more about last night, I grin at them both and spin round, heading into the lesson.

Seb taps me gently on the shoulder, but I pretend I haven't noticed and slip into my seat next to Louise.

When I look up, Seb is watching me from across the room, the crease across his brow deep and dark.

***

Thirty minutes into our biology lesson, I can't concentrate on a word Ms Greenwood is saying. Her high, lilting voice keeps drifting in and out of my consciousness. I stare at the laminated desk in front of me, trying to focus on her explanation of plant cells. I actually quite like biology, but every few seconds my eye is caught by my phone, which keeps lighting up with new notifications.

Louise wrinkles her nose and glances at the screen. 'He's keen.'

I raise my eyebrows but don't say anything. To be honest, my stomach is still feeling slightly queasy.

Sven hasn't stopped messaging since this morning, and I haven't sent a single one. After he called me a slut, he sent about six messages in a row apologizing, saying things like, *I don't know what came over me* and *I just hated the thought of you being with another guy.*

But despite his apologies, I couldn't bring myself to reply. It was fun before: I could imagine someone who thought I was beautiful; someone who was always there in my pocket to flirt with; someone to make me feel better about Tom.

But I didn't know him. Not really. He was just words on my phone, not a person I could trust. Reading through my messages made me realize how much I'd opened up to a complete stranger – how vulnerable I'd been. And I felt scared.

This morning, he's messaged me even more than usual.

Picking up old jokes we shared, sending me photos of things he's up to. I gnaw on my thumbnail.

Since I started first period biology, he's sent twenty-three messages.

Louise is now squinting down at her phone, scrolling through my Instagram profile.

'God, Sven's commented on every picture.' She rolls her eyes.

My stomach drops. *Every single picture?*

'Mmm,' I say, staring down at my textbook.

Louise shoots me a look. 'I mean, he's hot and everything, but that is weird.'

There's a second where I don't know what to say back, but then I just shrug.

'Yeah, he's obsessed.' I try to keep my voice even, but there's a slight tremor on the last word. I clear my throat.

Louise doesn't seem to have noticed. 'So what happened with your guy at the party? A couple of the others said you left together.'

I take a few seconds to finish annotating the cell I'm drawing, then look back at Louise with a puzzled expression.

'Who? Oh, that guy.' I wrinkle my nose. 'Yeah, he was all right. Nothing happened – he was a bad kisser and I was so out of it.'

Louise looks at me for a moment, then glances back at her phone, which has a message from Jerome.

'What happened with Jerome?' I say politely.

Louise's face breaks into a smile, before she quickly rearranges her features.

'Yeah, same really, I was so out of it, I left early, but he's been messaging.'

63

She holds out her phone to show me a string of messages between them, her chin jutting out.

I wrinkle my brow. 'Wasn't he dating that girl in the year below – Maisie or someone?'

'Oh no – that is *so* over,' she says with a snort, scrolling through her phone. 'Look, he even triple-messaged at one point!'

For some reason, even looking at those messages from Jerome on Louise's phone makes my stomach churn.

'Mmm . . . cool,' I mutter and put my head back to my textbook.

Louise is smirking down at her screen, then she glances at me. 'You OK?'

'What? Yeah – why?'

'You just seem, I dunno . . . quiet.'

I pause.

*What am I doing?* She's one of my best friends. I can tell her anything. *Anything*.

'Sorry, I should have . . .' I take a deep breath. 'Something else happened at the party—'

Louise gasps loudly and shakes her head.

'Don't Chlo – you don't have to say. I already know!'

I blink. 'You know?'

'Yes, Rachel saw.'

'Rachel *saw*?'

Louise nods. 'She saw everything.' She glances at my stricken expression. 'It's OK! He's a bastard. We all know he's a bastard.'

I nod dumbly. Feeling the colour drain from my face. They saw me and J. Louise – she knew? Everyone knows? Oh Christ. What do they all think of me?

64

Sven's message dances before my eyes.

**Sven_247** Slut.

Why the hell did I ever wear that stupid tight green dress? I thought I looked so pretty – now I wish I could screw it up into a tiny ball, rip the beaded material to shreds.

'. . . and to think he got with Tori, when you were right there—'

*Tori?* Wait, what—

Louise hasn't noticed my change of expression. She's talking fast, in a low, conspiratorial tone.

'It was his party, but c'mon. You've barely been split up a month!'

The churning in my stomach starts to ease. So no one actually saw me and J?

'Tom? Tom got with Tori? That's what you saw?'

Louise frowns at me. 'Um, yeah. Why, what did you think—'

'Oh, nothing. I just – it's just been *such* a shock, you know.'

Louise presses her lips together and squeezes my arm. 'I know. We can just be us girls at break if you want.'

'No, no. I'm going to have to talk to him at some point. Might as well clear the air.'

I'm slowly starting to digest the fact that Tom got with someone else. I expected to feel upset, but instead I just feel . . . numb.

Of course he was going to get with someone else. Look what I did – flirting with anyone in the room. He probably hates me.

I think of J's hands all over my body. My body tenses up.

To be honest, I hate myself.

Louise misinterprets my silence and gives me a sympathetic smile.

'*He's a dickhead,*' she mouths, reaching over and squeezing my arm.

I manage a weak smile back, as my phone lights up with three new messages.

***

At break, I find myself standing near one of the school benches along the tarmacked edge of the field, staring up at Tom's face.

I'm not quite sure how I ended up with just him. As soon as I approached the group of guys, all the girls went silent and Louise nudged me sharply in the ribs before saying, 'Tom, Chloe wants a word,' in an icy voice.

So now we're standing here. Alone.

Tom is fidgeting like he doesn't want to be here. I'm trying hard to ignore the heavy feeling of my phone in my pocket, vibrating manically against my leg.

Tom's floppy blond hair is more tousled than usual, and there are purple rings under his eyes.

He pouts.

After a few seconds of me not saying anything, he starts to bite one of his nails. 'Look. There's really not much to say, is there? You got with that guy from Andy's football team. I got with Tori. I know we were together a while, but –' he shrugs – 'we should at least try to be mates.'

Tom is looking down at me, his brow creased on his lightly tanned face.

66

'Right?'

My phone buzzes again against my leg. All of a sudden, I want to fall straight into Tom's chest, feel his familiar arms wrapped around me.

I feel so alone.

*BuzzBuzzBuzz.*

So scared.

'Chloe?' Tom's voice is gruff.

I swallow a hard lump in my throat.

'I'm going to head back to the guys. OK?'

Hot tears are welling in my eyes.

My phone buzzes again, and I feel one of the brimming tears splash down my cheek.

Tom ducks his head down to peer at me. I turn my head away, but he sees my face.

'Christ. What's wrong?'

Then his voice softens. He gently touches my shoulder.

'Are you OK?'

I look up at his kind face. Too good for me. I don't deserve him.

*BuzzBuzzBuzz.*

Tears erupt down my cheeks, and my whole body falls apart.

# CHAPTER 14

# Chloe

I can't stop crying. I don't mean I can't stop a pretty, single tear falling down my cheek. I mean I can't stop these huge chest-heaving sobs from racking my entire body.

I can't even speak. I'm trying to say something to Tom but all that is coming out is choking gasps. I can barely even breathe through the sobs.

Tom has seen me like this once, maybe twice before. When my mum threw me out of the house for coming home late a few months ago and I had nowhere to go. When my grandma died last year. He held me then, and I clung to him for comfort. It felt like things would never get better, but they did.

'Look, it's OK. Let's go somewhere private.' Tom takes my arm now, firmly, and steers me away from school.

I keep my head down, terrified someone else is going to see me in this state, but Tom leads me away from the crowds.

He takes me down the back path, by the humanities block, away from the main field. A couple of Year Sevens are loitering on the walkway. Before they catch a glimpse of me, he shouts at them to leave. They scatter like a flock of birds.

Once we reach the end of the path, he glances both ways to see if there are any teachers, before pulling me across the staff car park and out of the school gates. Tom can sign out without much trouble as he's in lower sixth, but if I'm caught walking out of school without permission, I'll be given detention for the rest of term.

A few steps past the school gates, Tom glances over his shoulder and waves me to sit down next to him on a low brick wall at the front of someone's garden.

My breath is still coming in huge, choking sobs, but there are no more tears. I'm just howling.

Tom digs his hands into his pockets. 'Fuck. I don't have a tissue.'

Almost without thinking about it, I lean my face against his chest. He wraps his arms around me and the warmth of his skin under his crisp white school shirt makes a tingling feeling sweep across my cheeks. His familiar smell takes me back to all the time we spent together.

I cry even harder.

*I just want everything to feel better.*

I've left black mascara marks and dirty foundation smudges across his shirt. I remember how nice it felt when we were together, kissing, skin on skin. I'm desperate to feel like that again.

Reaching my head up, I see Tom's concerned face and I press my lips against his. The warm sensation of his lips is so nice, I never want to think about anything else again.

Tom pushes me away abruptly. 'What are you doing?'

I blink several times. My bottom lip trembles. 'You don't . . . You don't want—' I can feel my throat choking again.

'What is going on with you? Why are you being like this? *You* split up with *me*, remember?'

My phone buzzes again against my leg.

I feel mad, unhinged.

Reaching into my pocket, I see over fifty messages from Sven, and in a blind fury I draw back my arm to throw the phone in the road.

Tom reaches above my head and grabs my wrist, holding it steady.

'I can't do this any more, Tom. I can't make him stop. Or the guy from the party. I can't make anyone stop.'

Tom looks at me and gently lets go of my wrist, taking my phone out of my hand. He glances down at the screen.

'Bloody hell. Who sends fifty messages in a morning?'

I snatch my phone back, embarrassed. I don't know why, but suddenly I feel like an idiot. Oh God, why did I burst into tears in front of Tom?

*Why am I behaving like this?*

'It's fine,' I say, flipping the phone screen over so neither of us can see. 'It's totally fine. I'm sorry – I don't know what came over me. I should have—' I try to keep my voice steady, but it cracks on the final word.

Slowly, Tom wraps an arm over my shoulder.

'What happened?' he says quietly.

I bury my head into his neck.

'I don't . . . I don't want to say,' I whisper.

Tom rests his lips against my forehead. 'Go on. Tell me.'

I swallow – my throat is so dry, and scratchy.

71

'It's that guy, Sven. I don't know – everyone.' My voice is so quiet, even I can barely hear it. 'And that guy J at the party, when we got together. I didn't want to – not once we got outside. He made me.'

Tom presses me tighter against his chest, and I grip onto the collar of his shirt.

# CHAPTER 15

## *Amber*

The air has turned bitingly cold by the time I'm walking back home from school. The wind clatters together a couple of coke cans rolling at the side of the road, and occasionally they brush against the pavement with a rattle.

My schoolbag is bumping against my back, and with each dull, rhythmic thud, my entire body cringes. I can't stop thinking about me pretending to be Ren's sister to the leisure centre people. It was so stupid.

*Why did I do it?*

My eyes skim over the group of Year Tens in front. They're all laughing, jostling into one another, and don't even notice me walking behind them.

I try to hang back a little so I don't end up directly beside them.

Ahead of the crowd, there's a flash of blue and orange sweatshirt on a tall, dark-haired guy.

Wait a minute—

Is that . . . *Ren*?

I crane my neck, but the figure is already heading down smokers' lane, this narrow, sloped walk between two of the housing estates. No one actually smokes there any more, but it still has the name.

Wait. What did I *actually* see?

It was only a flash of blue; a dash of orange. I tap open Snap Map, but Ren's not online. There's no way to know for sure.

Biting my lip, I quicken my pace.

\*\*\*

I've never been down smokers' lane before. I've never had a reason to; it comes out on the complete opposite side of town, and the only places I really visit are home, school and the gym.

A group of sixth-formers are standing at the entrance, but I don't even look at them. I stare at the ground, my cheeks prickling, and keep going. I feel like at any moment someone is going to turn around and tell me I'm not meant to be going this way. But they don't.

When I emerge at the bottom of the lane, Ren isn't there.

It's colder here, and the streets are flanked either side by blocks of flats, not houses. As I squint, there's a blob of royal blue in the far distance, snaking down the road.

Pulling my jumper down over my fingertips, I walk as fast as humanly possible in its direction. My teeth start to chatter, but I ignore it. Soon, I'm close enough to make out broad shoulders, a lick of dark hair at the nape of a neck.

*Oh-my-God. It's actually him.*

His phone buzzes, so he reaches in his pocket, turning his

head slightly. But it's the wrong face. His hair sticks directly up, and he has a flat, upturned nose.

Oh God, it's not Ren! It's one of the other college trainees from the gym. The one who's always talking to Ren. What was this guy's name – Ansh?

My stomach plummets. Here I am, in the middle of nowhere, behind some random guy who I don't know.

What am I *doing*?

I almost feel like I'm going to cry, but then something inside me stirs. This guy worked with Ren – he will know why he was fired. Maybe I could ask him what happened . . .

It takes me about a nanosecond to quicken my pace. Soon I'm standing directly beside him.

'Hey,' I say.

But he doesn't even hear me; he just walks on, staring ahead.

'Hey!' I say, a little louder this time.

He glances across at me, and I can feel myself give this weird, crooked smile. Ansh frowns slightly, his nose turning up even more.

'Have you just come from the gym?' I squeak.

He ducks his gangly head down and pulls one of his wireless headphones out of an ear.

'Are you speaking to me?' he says, dark eyes squinting.

'Yes, um, sorry . . .' I gulp. 'I, erm, recognized you – from the gym.'

'Oh,' he says, then he gives me a little half-smile, bending down to peer closer. 'Yeah, I think I've seen you around.'

There's a long pause.

'Are you walking this way too?' he says eventually, straightening up again.

I meet his eye and flush. 'Yeah, um – yeah, I am.'

We walk for a few steps. I open my mouth. Close it. Then open it again.

'So . . . do you . . . do you know . . .' I stare at my hands. 'Do you know why Ren doesn't work at the gym any more?'

Ansh looks at me. 'You're his sister, right?'

*How does he . . . ?*

'I was just chatting to the receptionist, who said Ren's sister had come by,' he says, as though he can read the question on my face.

I swallow. Here I go again.

'Yeah. Yeah, I am.'

# CHAPTER 16

# *Amber*

Ansh is looking down at me, the spikes of his dark gelled hair twitching in the wind. He frowns, and the edge of his lips crease.

'You don't know? Christ, sorry. I can't say – not to his sister.' He rakes a hand through his stiff hair.

I open my mouth, and before I know what's happening, I start talking. Quickly. Confidently. It's like I've stepped out of my own body and I'm listening to someone else. I hear her say some crap about how Ren won't stop talking about being fired at home; how Mum is totally stressed out. This other person says to Ansh they just want to hear what he thinks, as their brother's friend.

When I close my mouth, Ansh is looking at me with an odd expression on his face. He stops walking for a second.

'You're his sister . . . He never—'

'Me and my parents really, *really* want to hear what the other people at the gym think.'

Ansh lets out a low sigh. 'OK. If you want my honest o
pinion: I think he did it.'

'Did what?'

Ansh splays his hands out. 'Well, the first one – Maisie . . .
Was that her name? She said he never left her alone. Then he
turned up at her house one day.'

I blink several times.

'Ren turned up at someone's home?' I say quietly.

*How can I blame him for that, when I did the same?*

But it's almost like Ansh hasn't heard me; he keeps going.
'And then Jemma. He was always weird with her in the gym – he
did the same thing. And on the first day of October, they met
up – for a date, I guess. And –'Ansh shrugs. 'Well I guess no one
really knows what happened. He says they never met up. She
says that he, well . . .'

There's an icy feeling that runs down my spine. What is Ren
meant to have done, exactly . . .

*. . . And am I just as bad?*

Ansh sees my face. 'Are you OK?'

I shake my head. 'Yeah, I guess. It's just a lot to take in.'

Ansh runs a hand across the back of his skinny neck. 'Didn't
you say you and your family knew about this already?'

'Um, I did,' I say quickly. 'Just not the details. My – er – our
parents didn't say.'

Ansh raises his eyebrows. 'Good. Glad I don't have to tell you
the last story then. It's grim.'

'What do you mean—'

'Here's me,' says Ansh, nodding to an alley that leads to about
four houses.

78

I can't really pretend I need to go that way too; he must know I don't live in one of those houses . . . Maybe I could say I've just moved in? I doubt he knows his neighbours very well . . .

'Catch you later,' he says, before I have time to say anything, and he gives me a wave.

I want to ask him more questions, but I can't think of a normal way to do it, so I just stare dumbly at him as he walks off.

My mind is buzzing.

So Ren turned up at Maisie's house, and then did something that upset Jemma on their date. Why would that get him fired?

And what happened to the third girl?

I think of the way Ren smiled at me, his hand gently resting on my shoulder. I try to imagine him turning up at Maisie's house . . . but he just wouldn't do things like that – I'm sure of it.

The wind rattles, and a shiver snakes down my spine.

There's something else that's been bothering me since I heard he met up with Jemma. Something feels off.

I think back to last night, lying in bed, scrolling through Ren's Instagram feed.

*Wait a minute . . .*

I unlock my phone, exit Snap Map, and click on to his Instagram profile. I scroll back further, to the beginning of October.

On 01 October at 9.01 p.m., there's an Instagram video he's posted of him on the sofa with several mates drinking beers.

There's a tiny caption: *Great night in with the lads.*

***

He wasn't out that night on a date with Jemma. He was with his friends.

Frowning, I click through to Jemma's Instagram. There's nothing there, so I scroll through a couple of her friends' profiles, hoping to spot a clue from that night.

On one girl's page, Ope, there's a shot of Jemma with her arms wrapped around a tall, dark-haired guy I don't recognize. Date posted: 01 October.

I try to click through to this guy's profile, but he's not tagged. Even in the out-of-focus image, I can tell one thing: that man is *not* Ren.

I knew it! He couldn't have done those things.

But if he didn't go after those girls, why does everyone think he did? I gnaw on my inner lip until the skin grows sore.

*Has Ren been set up?*

# CHAPTER 17

## Chloe

The rest of the day, me and Tom don't go back to school – we keep walking. We go through the main high street, along the arcades, past the town church, down by the river.

I know I look a mess. I can feel my make-up smeared across my face, see half of it smudged on Tom's shirt, but he doesn't even seem to notice.

We're walking along the paths we used to take when we first started dating, holding hands. There's something about his skin on mine that makes me feel so much safer, so much less alone. Every so often, tears prick the back of my eyes, and I let them spill down my cheeks. I sniff into the sleeve of my school jumper and dab the black marks across the hem of navy blue.

Me and Tom are tracing our steps now along the pavement by his house. We didn't even plan it – just followed our feet. His family are actually nice, so we never went to mine when we were together. Mum would just make things difficult.

Tom smiles now as we get closer to his house.

'You know my parents nearly killed me this morning.'

I look up, and his eyes crinkle.

'Apparently someone sat on the cooker, and now it needs replacing. I'm having to repay them in instalments.'

'Tell me that doesn't mean more car wash?'

The 'car wash' is what Tom calls his job at the petrol station, because almost every shift someone can't work the self-service car wash at the side and asks him to come out and wash the car for them. Several times, he's tried to explain he doesn't wash cars, or he's tried to take the pump off irate customers and ended up getting soaked.

He lifts his eyes to the sky. 'Yes. Double shift at the car wash. Better bring my trunks.'

I start laughing weakly, and he smiles.

My phone starts buzzing again, and my body tenses up.

'Ohhh!' I groan, dropping Tom's hand and pulling out the screen. 'Why won't he stop messaging me?'

'Let me have a look.' Tom takes the phone off me.

As we walked along the town, I told him everything about what happened when I left the party, but I only mentioned Sven briefly. Part of me was worried how he would react. Me and Sven had been messaging every minute – I even called him late at night. I know Tom and I weren't together, but part of me feels . . . I don't know what.

Tom frowns, flicking through the most recent messages and my non-responses.

'Christ. Sending that many messages without a response isn't normal.'

Hearing Tom say that makes me start to relax.

But there's something else I need to get off my chest.

'Me and Sven—'

Tom looks at me.

'. . . We, erm, messaged this morning after the thing happened with that J-guy.'

A flicker of annoyance passes over Tom's features.

'He – he called me a *slut*.'

The word hangs in the air between us.

'I just . . . I feel –' I take a deep breath. 'Do you think that's what I am?'

Tom takes a long, deep sigh.

'For God's sake, stop being ridiculous. What is this guy – from the 1950s? You can do whatever you want. He said that because he likes you. He'd call you a slut if you got with anyone apart from him. Why are you even talking to him?'

'I don't kn—' But before I can finish the sentence, it clicks into place.

*Because I'm scared.*

But of what, exactly? This is a guy I've never met. He probably wouldn't even recognize me in real life. Why have I been replying to him just because he might freak out again?

'You're right,' I say instead.

Feeling some of my old resolve trickle back, I look at the fifty unanswered messages – and delete him from my WhatsApp. Then I go into settings, enter his contact, and click *block calls and texts from this number*.

Tom raises his eyebrows. 'Not even going to tell him why?'

But I'm already feeling lighter, more free. My phone isn't buzzing – and it's not going to. Unless there's a message from someone I know.

'He can work it out.' I slip my phone into my pocket, and look up to see Tom still watching me.

'I've missed you, you know,' he says quietly, playing with the strap of his backpack. 'I know you made the decision, but, yeah, it was tough.'

I think of the last month away from him. How angry I was – but also how alone and vulnerable I felt. How I tried to fill the void with other people, and Sven, which worked . . . for a while.

I think back to the party, me flirting with everyone there.

'I'm sorry.' I look up at him. 'I'm so, so sorry. About everything. I know you probably won't forgive me, that there's nothing I can do to take it back. But I want you to know – I know I was wrong. I made a mistake . . .' There's a lump forming in my throat. 'I miss you too.'

Tom doesn't take long to respond. He puts his arms around my small shoulders and pulls me into him. Not greedily, like J, but gently. I can feel my heart filling up, and I feel the weight of everything I did crashing down on me.

I should never have broken up with Tom. I was so difficult – such an idiot. Why am I like this? Why did I go around flirting with everyone in front of him? Why can't I just be *nice*?

'I love you,' I say, slipping back into our old language without even meaning to. I look up in shock, wanting to take the words back, but Tom is looking down at me with a strange expression.

He looks annoyed, but his eyes are very wide.

Tom sighs.

'I never stopped,' he says quietly, and our lips meld into one.

# CHAPTER 18

## Amber

When I get in from school, Mum is busy making pasta in the kitchen, but other than the gentle bubbling of boiling water, the house is oddly quiet. I go straight up to my room, fling open the door, and almost jump out of my skin when I see the tall figure of Seb sitting hunched over the edge of my bed, gently tapping a football between his two big feet.

My eyes dart to my laptop, but it's closed and off.

'What are you doing in my room?!' I shout.

Seb looks up.

He doesn't say anything. Instead, he goes back to staring at the ground and nudging the football between his two feet.

I approach him gingerly and see there's a deep crease between his two brows.

'Are – are you OK?'

He shrugs, his bottom lip sticking out.

'Yeah,' he says.

But it's not the usual laughing, joking Seb. There's a flatness to his voice. I've only seen him like this a handful of times: that summer he broke his leg and couldn't see any of his friends, and when Dad shut him in his room all weekend for breaking my bike when we were eight. Essentially, any time you cut Seb off from his many friends, it's like his entire mood gets drained.

I take a step forward. 'Why aren't you chatting to Will? Or Andy or someone?'

Seb looks up at me, and there's a half-smile playing on his lips. 'It's Bill, you idiot,' he says, but softly.

Then he sighs and leans backwards flat on my bed, his big hands covering his face.

'Uggggggggh.'

'What?'

He looks up to the ceiling for a moment, thoughtful, biting his lip. Then his frowning eyes meet mine.

'You know Chloe—'

'MacNeil?'

'Yeah. Well you know that party I was at last night—'

There's a small pang in my chest. I didn't even know he was at a party. I'd assumed he was at late-night football training at his friend's house because that's what he'd told Mum.

'Um, yeah.'

'Well I came back about midnight, and I saw this dark-haired guy – one of Andy's friends . . . I've played him at football before. He was there, with Chloe –' Seb sticks out his bottom lip – 'and I tried not to look, because, y'know, I'm pissed. But then I saw him pushing her against a tree. I think . . . I think she was trying to get away. So I went over, but she shoved him and ran off before I got close.'

Seb is staring, hard, at the ground. There's an awkward pause as my eyes flicker over his face. He shakes his head and sighs bitterly.

'I tried to speak to her at school, she says it's nothing, but, like . . . it didn't look like nothing.'

Seb kicks the football gently at my shins. But I can barely focus – my mind has just realized something. Something big. Something that makes complete sense.

'What was the guy's name?'

'What?'

'The guy who got with Chloe, you said he had dark hair – what was his name?'

Seb is shaking his head. 'I don't . . . Why do you—'

'Please!' I look at Seb, my eyes wide. 'I think there might be two victims here.'

# CHAPTER 19

## *Chloe*

The next few days pass in a blur of long walks and laughter. When we get back to school on Monday, each day I'm desperately itching to get through lessons so I can go back out on the field and see Tom. It's not like before, when we first went out and stood at the edge of the field where everyone could see us. This time, I walk with him at the back of the school grounds, away from everyone, so we can just stand together, kiss, and talk.

Everyone wants to know what's going on with us, but I couldn't feel less like talking about it. Louise, Rachel, Ameerah have all messaged me in the last few days, or grabbed me in lessons asking for the gossip, but I've been vague about me and Tom 'needing time to work things out'.

The truth is I don't feel like I normally do. I don't feel like speaking to anyone, to be honest. And I don't want to get worried about other girls and get carried away, like I did before.

After school on Wednesday, I'm round at Tom's, and we're lying on his bed: me propped up on my elbows, and him on his back, tracing his fingertips across my shoulders. I'm beginning to feel myself relax for the first time in weeks.

I lay my head across his chest as he laughs at some memes he's scrolling through on his phone. He occasionally shows them to me, and I smirk. We're not even talking about anything really, just lying together, laughing, occasionally kissing – but I feel like I'm home again.

It doesn't matter if Mum screams at me or if Louise is being moody – I have Tom, my best friend, back.

All of a sudden, Tom frowns at his phone. I loll my head against his chest.

'What's up?'

He seems to notice me for the first time and changes his expression.

'Oh, what? Nothing. Just a meme I didn't get.'

Something in his tone makes me frown.

'Show me?'

He shrugs. 'Nah, I've scrolled past it now –' he shows me his phone, which is open on an Instagram photo from LADbible – 'I'll never find it again.'

'Oh, OK.' I pick up my own phone and open Instagram. There's twenty notifications I haven't looked at.

Tom's eyes widen as I scroll through my pictures.

'You know what we should do,' he says, gently taking my phone out of my hands. 'Let's post a selfie.'

'A *selfie*?'

'Yeah. Of us – why not? Show people we're back together.'

Tom has never suggested posting a selfie before.

'We've only been dating a few days. Don't you think it's a bit . . . soon?'

I think of Sven and how he will react. I can't bear to think of how many unseen messages have been silently filling up on my phone from his blocked number. But surely he must have gotten the idea by now. It's been several days. He's probably stopped messaging, hasn't he? I know I would if someone ghosted me.

Then again, maybe a selfie with Tom is a good thing. Show I'm not interested.

Maybe Tom is the one who wants to make this clear.

'OK, sure,' I say.

Tom smiles. 'Here we go.'

He takes my phone, clicks on the front camera, and very deliberately leans down in view of the screen, placing a kiss on my forehead. I pull a closed-lip smile and turn to show my better side. After a couple of takes, I glance at the screen. It's very coupley. Very obvious. You wouldn't post a photo of your friend or your brother kissing your forehead like that.

I dither for a few moments. Tom glances at me.

Oh, screw it. We *are* back together. Who cares what Sven thinks? If anything, it'll get him off my case.

I post the photo with a love-heart emoji, and Tom immediately likes it, commenting with a kissing-face smiley.

Louise, Ameerah and about fifteen others from school quickly react with likes and hearts.

I snuggle back down next to Tom, and he pulls me right on top of him, making me giggle.

'There. It's on Instagram now – it's official,' he says, kissing my nose.

I kiss his face back, smiling.

\*\*\*

Later that night, after Tom has walked me back to my house, I'm lying in bed, staring at the phone screen when I get a ding from Instagram. Idly, I click through to the notification.

It's a new comment on one of my photos. From Sven.

I already know which photo it'll be. It only takes a few seconds for the photo of Tom kissing the top of my head to load into view.

I scroll down, biting at a hangnail.

**Sven_247** *WHORE.*

The phone screen swims in front of me.

Dumbly, I click through my other unread notifications. I didn't pay much attention to them earlier, but now I see all the comments he's posted – about five on every photo.

**Sven_247** *Looking stunning, beautiful.*
**Sven_247** *My baby <3*
**Sven_247** *Can't wait to speak to you later, my baby <3*

I stare at the comments, my mouth open. Anyone would think we were dating. No one would think from his words that this is just some guy I messaged a few times on WhatsApp and called once.

Is this what Tom saw on my Instagram tonight? Is *this* why he wanted us to post a photo?

There's a sinking feeling in my stomach as I get another notification. A new comment from Sven on the photo of me and Tom.

Three words.

**Sven_247** *Who is he?*

# CHAPTER 20

## Amber

On Saturday morning, every screen I own is spread out across the kitchen table, open on images of Ren. My hair is in a messy bun, and tendrils keep flicking down across my face as my eyes skim across his Facebook, Instagram, Twitter and Snapchat.

I still can't work out what's really going on. It's like a stubborn stain I can't scrub out. My mind keeps circling back to Ansh's words. Trying to understand what he meant – trying to find anything that could give me more of a clue as to what Ren did, or what he is meant to have done.

I scratch the side of my nose and a flop of hair falls across my face. I tuck it behind one ear and my eyes flit between the screens.

I'm going to keep going until I get to the bottom of this. So far, I've noted down his location every time he's shared it on Snap Map. From searching his Facebook friends, I've discovered he (luckily) has two sisters. He's the middle child, with one older sister and one about my age, judging by his mum's Instagram photos.

He started training as a personal trainer with the local college on 4 October. Since then, he seems to have gathered loads of good reviews on the leisure centre's Facebook page.

I glance down at the Google doc I've started. I'm linking up every date the girls have accused him of something with posts from his Instagram and Facebook. The problem is, I only know the date for the second girl, Jemma. The others are still a mystery.

At that moment, Mum comes bustling into the kitchen with a huge basket of washing in her outstretched arms. I quickly swipe and click my screens over to my maths homework.

'Hey.' Mum smiles as she plops a load of washing on the kitchen worktop and starts bundling it into the machine. 'Want to give me a hand?'

I get up and start helping her. She's so pretty, my mum. She has this shock of long, wavy dark hair, which tumbles down across her face as she shoves the clothes in the machine. As I pass crumpled balls of clothes to her, she sticks out her tongue in concentration.

Mum is like Seb. She's friends with everyone, knows everyone. And she's lived in our town since she was a teenager. Sometimes it feels like she knows more people my age than I do.

'Mum?' I say, putting my head on one side.

'Uh-huh,' she responds, shaking some powder into the top of the machine and only half listening, her tongue still slightly sticking out.

'Do you . . . You know . . . Have you ever heard of the Moore family?'

'The Moores?'

I glance up, but Mum has stopped doing the washing and has

already started walking out of the kitchen, back up the stairs. That's another way she's like Seb: she's always rushing to do something else; you can never quite catch her.

I start hurrying out of the kitchen, but I'm slower than Mum, and she's already at the top of the stairs. By the time I get there, she's disappeared into Seb's bedroom.

'So, do you remember, um, the Moores?' I say, casually leaning against the doorframe to his room. Mum is busy folding dry clothes, so I take them from her.

She smiles.

'Mm . . . the Moores? Oh! The ones with the little boy and two girls – one about your and Seb's age? The other in college? Well she must be out of college now, probably grown up, with her own job and—'

I cut her off. 'Yes. Them. Do you know anything more about . . .' I pause, trying to work out how to phrase this. 'I spoke to Ren the other day, in the gym. I think that was their son, but I wasn't sure. Do you remember the family? Was he . . . nice?'

'Nice?' Mum wrinkles her nose, then gives a little laugh. 'You ask such strange questions sometimes! Yes, he was nice. Fine! They all were. Well . . .' She glances at me. 'Well he did have a bit of trouble at school, from what I can remember, but I think that got sorted out.'

'Trouble? What kind of trouble? Did he seem like the type to – did he – did we get on? When we were kids, I mean—'

At that moment, there's an ear-splitting ring from the telephone on the stand beside us. Both of us nearly jump out of our skin.

'Your bloody father and his hearing!' mutters Mum, grabbing the phone before it explodes both of our ears again.

95

She immediately starts chatting animatedly into the receiver. I flick my eyes to the ceiling and turn round. Slowly I make my way back down the stairs.

Great. I found out absolutely nothing, apart from that Ren may or may not have been a bit of trouble at school when he was five.

As I'm tracing my feet down the soft steps, the back door rattles. Seb is bounding in through the kitchen. There's the familiar sound of water trickling from the tap, the bash of cupboards rapidly opening and closing, then silence.

I glance back up the stairs. Maybe later, when she's had a glass of wine, I can ask Mum about Ren again. She might not tell me anything new – but every little thing is useful at this stage.

Seb's loud, deep voice echoes up from the kitchen, vibrating through the walls.

'Amber! What the hell have you been looking at?'

A trickle of ice runs down my spine.

I bolt downstairs so fast, even Mum can't catch me up.

# CHAPTER 21

# Amber

When I reach the kitchen, Seb is standing there, holding my phone in his hand and squinting at my laptop screen. He's closed down my maths homework page to reveal multiple tabs of Ren's social media accounts.

'No, no, no!' I scream, trying manically to grab the tablet off him and slam the laptop shut.

He steps out of the way but stands up, holding them out of my reach.

'Christ,' he says, his eyes skimming the tabs. 'Someone's got a serious crush.'

'No – don't!'

I've got the laptop shut now, tucked under my arm, but I make another grab for my phone. He holds it out of the way and starts reading from one of Ren's Instagram captions.

'*Deadlifted 100kg at the gym last night. Buzzing*,' Seb reads out drily. 'Oh man, what a lad.' He starts reading more of them, in a stupid, high-pitched voice, collapsing with laughter each time.

My life is spiralling out of control. I can see Seb telling Mum, Dad, everyone at school. I can see people thinking I'm even more of a freak than I am now. I won't be able to find out anything else about Ren getting fired – people will just think I have this stupid girly crush.

My knees slip to the floor as Seb keeps reading out the captions. Now he's started doing muscle-man poses and laughing loudly at his own jokes. I put my head in my hands.

Tears prick the back of my eyes. For the first time in I-don't-know-how-long, I felt like I was actually doing something important. I was looking forward to going to school tomorrow to find out more about what was going on. I felt like . . . I don't know . . .

Like I had a *purpose*.

Seb has stopped talking now. I blink hard, trying not to cry, but a tear leaks out and courses down my cheek. I brush it away roughly.

After a couple of seconds, I feel a rough squeeze on my shoulder. Seb is bent over, staring down at me.

'Hey.' His voice has changed now. It's not stupid and high-pitched; it's low and soft. When I look up, his brow is knitted together. 'Sis. Don't be like that. It's OK – everyone stalks people. You think I haven't looked at Chloe's Instagram? Danny has made a whole bank of –' He shakes his head suddenly, like he's just realized he's speaking to me and not one of his mates. 'You all right?'

I turn my head away from him. 'I'm not – I'm not stalking him,' I say, my voice so quiet, even I can't hear it. 'I'm . . . I think he was framed. I'm trying to help.'

When I look up, Seb's lips are pursed on one side. 'He was *framed*?'

'Yeah, um—' It sounds so stupid saying any more out loud that I just shut up. As we're looking at each other, there's the thud of Mum coming down the stairs.

My eyes widen. I take my phone off Seb, and he doesn't put up a fight.

'Don't – please don't tell Mum,' I say, my eyes swivelling upwards.

Seb almost looks uncomfortable. Then he gives my shoulder another squeeze and smiles with his lips closed. 'Don't worry.'

He starts walking past me, back into the hallway. As he leaves the kitchen, he turns back. 'If you really think that dick Ren Moore is innocent, though, you might want to read Jemma Okeke's Facebook post first.'

My mouth falls open. Seb knows about Ren and the rumours? Well of course he does. He knows everyone. I'm not sure why I'm even surprised.

At that moment, Mum comes back into the kitchen. Quickly, I gather up my phone, laptop, tablet – lock the screens – and hurry out of the room.

*Jemma Okeke.*

The second girl who made a claim about him. She wrote about Ren? On her Facebook? As fast as I can, I start clicking through people's Facebook profiles until I find her. She's in the year above at school, in Year Twelve . . . but all her accounts are private.

With a sinking heart, I stare at the screen. I'm almost tempted to google how you hack into people's social media accounts, but

I bet I could never manage it. And it feels like doing that would cross some sort of invisible line.

At the bottom of her Facebook page, it says, *One mutual friend Sebastian Nighy.*

'Mum! Where are my stud boots?' shouts Seb from upstairs.

He's about to go out for football training, and he almost always leaves his Facebook signed in. As Seb bashes around in the hall, throwing every boot he can find out of the coat closet, I quietly slip upstairs.

I hover outside the door to his room. I can hear Seb ringing his friends, smashing his studded boots against the hard laminate floor in the hall, Mum screaming at him to put them on outside. Then I hear him skidding, clattering across the floor, shouting bye to Mum, and slamming the door shut in a cacophony of noise and colour.

Once he leaves, there's silence.

A prickling sensation sweeps across the back of my neck. Slowly, I start walking into Seb's room. If anyone asks why I'm in here, I'm looking to check my maths homework against his. Mum probably won't remember we're in different sets. I tiptoe towards his computer and tap the mouse to flicker on the screen. It's not locked.

I pull up Facebook.

In a couple of clicks, I'm on Jemma's page. There's the profile picture of her posing in the mirror that I've seen before – but now the whole page is full of comments, photos, statuses. I can see *everything*.

It doesn't take me long to find the status post I'd been searching for.

## BEWARE OF REN MOORE!

I went on a date with him, and it turned into the worst night of my life.

I never wanted to write this. I've written and deleted this post so many times, I've lost count, but now I've decided: I need to tell everyone the truth.

We met at the gym, at the start of school, and immediately hit it off. We messaged almost constantly for a few weeks before he asked me to the cinema.

I was so excited. It feels so stupid to say it now, but I was. The date went well. After the cinema, we were walking along the pavement, and he put his arm around me.

Then we found a little alcove by the bike railings, and he leaned down to kiss me. I didn't feel quite ready, but it was OK. I mean, I thought it was OK. After a couple of minutes, I tried to twist myself away, but he became forceful.

He grabbed my bum, my breasts. I laughed and shrugged him off. I feel like an idiot now, because I laughed. But I didn't know what else to do.

I said I wanted to go home, but he kept saying, 'No, we're having fun.' I think he thought I was teasing him. But I wasn't. He kept kissing me, holding my head still, even though I asked him to stop.

After the date, I told him I wasn't happy, that I didn't want to see him any more. He said I had led him on. He kept messaging me for weeks and weeks until I blocked him.

I wasn't sure if this story was worth sharing, when some people have so much worse experiences, but if it helps just one person feel less alone, then it's worth it.

I finish reading, and I feel like all the air has been punched out of my lungs.

# CHAPTER 22

## *Amber*

I realize I'd been gripping the edge of my chair so tightly while reading Jemma's post, I've left nail marks in the wood. I try to smudge them away with my palm, but they stay etched into the arm.

I scroll further down. Almost a hundred girls, most of whose names I recognize from school, have posted messages and reactions in the thread.

> **Joss Lang** *You are so brave for sharing this. I can't imagine what you've been through.*
> **Evie Fuller** *This is so, so important. You've exposed him and saved other girls from this fate.*
> **Mischa Thompson** *We all love you, Jemma. Stay strong, beautiful lady.*

There's a sick feeling in my stomach. I keep thinking of all these people, all condemning Ren . . . And yet, he *didn't* go on a date with her. At least not on October 1st, according to that Instagram post. He was staying in with his friends.

I keep trying to picture Jemma's story. Would Ren really be forceful like that? Ren was always so kind in the gym, rushing around, helping people.

But this isn't just one story. This is two girls – three, potentially.

I clutch my head in my hands.

How could *all three* girls get the wrong guy?

I scroll back through Jemma's Facebook page. I want to find that dark-haired guy again. The one she was with – does he play football? Could it possibly be the same guy who Seb saw with Chloe?

I've clicked back through her photos when I finally see him in the corner of a full-room house-party shot.

And he's tagged.

My heart gives a little leap.

Biting my lip, I click on his name.

*Jerome Femi.*

Damn! His account is private.

My eyes flick back to Jemma's status. There's got to be another clue. Something to prove she's got the wrong guy.

Scrolling through Jerome's Facebook, I realize not all his photos are private. There's a few pictures of him out with his mates, several with girls. In one, there's just him and another girl outside the multiplex cinema. Ansh Laghari has tagged them both with the caption *Lovebirds*.

There's a metallic taste in the back of my mouth as I hover over the girl's face.

Maisie Evans.

Maisie! The first girl. Something is seriously up here.

But whose photos are these?

*Ansh Laghari.*

Wait a minute. I know that name. I know that face.

It's *the* Ansh. From the gym. He'll know what really happened, won't he? He'll know whether Ren actually went on that date with Jemma, or whether it was Jerome.

Mum starts crashing around downstairs, so, with a jolt, I lock Seb's computer and tiptoe back into my room.

Sitting on the edge of my bed, I unlock my phone and open Ansh's Instagram, immediately clicking follow. Then I start typing out a message from my own account and, almost without thinking, hit send.

> **Amber0789** Hey, I was wondering, are you in the gym tomorrow?

I start to feel an uneasy clutch in my stomach. I shouldn't have sent that; it looks weird. Oh, God, what if he thinks I'm a complete and utter freak? What if he realizes I'm *not* Ren's sister? Also, there's nothing on Ren's profile about his sisters, but if Ansh thinks we're family, won't it look odd that Ren doesn't follow me, and I'm Nighy, while he's Moore?

No, it'll be fine. He'll never guess. My handle is Amber0789. I could be Amber Moore, for all he knows.

With a swallow, I click back to the tagged photo of Jerome with Maisie. It could be a coincidence. Maybe one of them just got their dates muddled?

Maybe he really *did* harass her.

Ren's kind face flashes before me. The way he gently brushed my shoulder; the prickling feeling that swept up my arm.

Whether he's innocent or guilty, I need to know.

# CHAPTER 23

## Chloe

I push the thought of Sven's messages to the back of my mind for the rest of the week, but every so often, when I'm not quite paying attention, one word rings in my ears.

*WHORE.*

After school on Friday, I'm standing in the sixth-form toilets, applying lipstick with Louise and Rachel, when my hand slips, and there's a tiny swipe of red on my front tooth. I sigh and start dabbing it off. We're about to go join the guys on this cornfield nearby, where we usually sip cider, and a couple of the guys bring Bluetooth speakers to play music and add to the atmosphere.

Usually, I love our Friday nights on the field, but tonight I keep ruining my make-up. My hand, no matter how long I take to draw on eyeliner or outline my lips, won't hold steady.

In the mirror, I survey my face with a critical eye.

My lips are too red. My eyeshadow isn't dark enough. My eyebrows are filled in, but too smudgy. My concealer is so thick, it's going cakey on top of my primer.

I almost want to dunk my head in water and scrub it all off. Go out to see everyone with black marks smeared all over my face and my gaping pores and whiteheads on full view – have everyone look in horror at my natural, imperfect face.

I let out a sigh, and Louise slides a glance at me as she applies mascara. She's barely said a word to me all day.

'Everything OK?' says Rachel.

'Yeah. I just can't get my sodding lips right.' I pout in front of the mirror and pull down my top so my cleavage stands out a bit more.

'Why don't you try mine?' says Rachel, nodding at her pale pink lipstick.

I carefully dab off my red lipstick with a tissue and start applying hers.

The problem is I can't stop thinking about all the comments Sven posted on my Instagram. *Baby Chloe <3* is the one that sends a shiver down my spine. I deleted them, of course. And reported him and blocked his account. But I can't scrub them out of my mind – not completely.

I bite my lip, which looks even worse with Rachel's pale pink lip colour, and reapply my dark red.

'Mm, think I prefer the red,' I say, smiling.

Louise doesn't smile back. I feel a flicker of annoyance, but then shake myself. She's just being Louise, and I'm being paranoid.

'Let's go.' I swing my bag over my shoulder and push open the door. At least tonight we'll all drink and laugh, and Tom will be there.

Everything will be fine.

\*\*\*

The evening passes in a blur of noise and colour. The guys keep being loud, showing off – everyone giggling, flirting. At one point, Tom plants a kiss on me in front of everyone, and I feel so light, so free, that I begin to slip back into my old self.

Sven doesn't even cross my mind as I take hundreds of photos of us all together – gathered in a circle, pouting at the camera, the girls huddled in front, and the guys behind, reaching their long arms up to the night sky. At one point, one of Tom's mates, Rishaan, lifts me right up onto his shoulders and starts spinning me round and round. I clutch onto his head, giggling madly, my long hair swinging either side of his face.

When he puts me down, Tom runs over and charges head first into me – nuzzling his happy eyes-half-closed face into my neck. I kiss his hairline and wrap my arms around him. He goes to kiss my lips, but that's not what I want to do in front of everyone. Not now.

My limbs uncoordinated, I untangle myself from him and flop down on the cool grass next to Louise. I've barely spoken to her all night, but now I pass her a cider and pick up another can. The night air is loud and warm with our laughter.

Louise is looking at the ground but struggling to hold her gaze. She's squinting so hard, her eyes look tiny and cat-like in the darkness.

'I've barely seen you tonight, girl,' I say, linking my arm in hers.

Louise's unfocused eyes lift to mine, but she doesn't respond.

The moonlight is reflecting across her pretty face, but there's a tightness in her jaw that the soft light can't hide.

She takes a sip of cider. 'Why did you do it?' she says quietly.

I frown. 'Do what?'

'Why did you get with him?'

'Who? Tom?' My thoughts are slow, foggy. It takes a second for my brain to catch up. 'That guy at the party? Joshua? John?'

Louise curls her lip. 'No! You know exactly who I'm talking about.'

My mouth falls open. 'What are you on about? You know everyone I've got with. I tell you everything. I don't know who you are talking about—'

'Look, if you're not going to tell me, that's fine,' cuts in Louise. 'But please, don't insult my intelligence.'

'Louise—'

She shakes her arm out of mine aggressively and tries to stand up, trips slightly, then starts walking off.

'Wait!' I stand up too fast, stumbling over my trainers. I grab her shoulders. 'You're just drunk. Stop. Stop!'

Louise turns round. In the moonlight, tears are glimmering in her eyes.

'You could get with anyone you wanted. Anyone,' she whispers. 'Why couldn't you have left him for me?'

Before I have a chance to speak, she storms off into the night.

As she disappears into some trees, there's a gargled sob.

I stand there dumbly as Rachel runs after her, and a couple of the guys start giggling.

My heart is thumping in my throat.

Louise knows everyone I've ever got with. I haven't hidden anything from her.

Tom comes over and puts an arm around my shoulder. 'Don't worry about it – she's just drunk.'

I think of the way she behaved today. How she barely even looked or spoke to me during every lesson together. I was so busy chatting to everyone else, I barely noticed, to be honest. But now I think about it, she's usually right by my side, in every conversation.

I frown at the spot where she stood.

*What is going on?*

# CHAPTER 24

# *Chloe*

On Monday when I come into school, Louise is huddled in a circle whispering to Rachel and Ameerah outside registration. I go over to join them, but instead of looking up, they fall silent.

Rachel shoots me a look. Louise won't even meet my eye.

'Hey,' I say, sidling next to them.

No one speaks.

I launch into talking about Friday night, but Louise coughs and looks the other way. Ameerah glances at the floor and starts fidgeting.

I look at all of them.

*What the hell?*

Louise stalks off to sit in her seat when I'm mid-story. As soon as she's out of earshot, I grab Rachel and Ameerah and pull them aside.

'OK, so something weird happened on Friday night,' I say in hushed tones, and then explain exactly what Louise said to me. 'It's just so bizarre. I don't know why she's being like this.'

But it doesn't get the reaction I was expecting. No one is gasping or saying Louise is acting strangely. They just . . . don't say anything.

Rachel gets two spots of pink on her cheeks and doesn't meet my eye. Ameerah frowns.

'Mmm,' says Rachel. She takes a deep breath. 'The thing is – The thing . . . I mean, are you sure you never got with Jerome?'

'Jerome!' I give a relieved laugh. 'That's who she thinks I got with? C'mon!'

'And that other guy you said – J,' says Ameerah.

The mention of him sends a jolt through my spine, which I brush aside.

I shake my head.

'You guys really think I got with Jerome? When? She's being silly. Look, I'll go and speak to Louise at break. Get this sorted out.'

But the girls aren't smiling and shaking their head at Louise. Instead, they're looking at me like they can't quite believe what they're hearing.

'Yeah, I really think you should speak to Louise,' says Ameerah quietly.

Our form tutor Ms Brown wanders over and waves us into our seats. When I get to me and Louise's desk, it's empty. I glance across the room. Louise has gone to sit in the spare seat beside Ameerah, and they're huddled with their heads together in an intense conversation.

I feel a heat spread across my cheeks.

*Fine. I don't need her.*

Lifting my chin, I push one of my long curls over my shoulder and sit down at the desk, alone. Then I pull out my phone and start messaging Tom. He almost instantly replies with a funny GIF, but it doesn't make me smile. I put down my phone and glance back at Louise.

I just don't understand what's going on. I never got with Jerome. I've barely even spoken to him. And I knew him and Louise were getting together, so I wouldn't have got with him.

So why does she think I did?

At that moment, there's a knock at the door. It's one of the Year Eleven prefects with her chin up, holding a scrap of square paper like her life depends on keeping it pristine.

I roll my eyes. She glances at me with what looks like a sneer, then says something to Ms Brown.

Ms Brown takes the paper, pushes her glasses to the end of her nose, and looks straight at me.

'Chloe MacNeil, Ms Benewood would like to see you. In her office.'

The headteacher's office?

'Ms Benewood would like to see *me*?'

'Yes. In her office. Now, please. We haven't got all day.'

A hush descends across the entire class. Every single eye is on me – and Louise gives a snort of laughter as I stand up. My cheeks are burning, and I can't meet anyone's eye.

I take a few steps towards Ms Brown.

'Why does she want to see me?' I say, lifting my chin.

Ms Brown's gaze scans over the class, who are all leaning forward, eager. 'I think it's best that she speaks to you about that,' is all she says.

As soon as I leave the classroom, I can hear everyone erupt into chatter. Ms Brown desperately tries to quieten them. 'OK, everyone – calm down,' she says about a million times.

I sigh and lean back against the cool wall outside class.

There's the loud sound of a throat being cleared. It's the prefect – Alison, or something. I can't quite remember her name.

I look up at her. 'Yes?'

'I'm here to escort you to Ms Benewood.'

'*Escort* me?'

'Yes.'

'Are you serious?'

But she doesn't reply; she just looks nervously from side to side.

*Oh, for God's sake.*

'OK, OK – I'm coming,' I say, and start walking ahead of her towards the headteacher's office.

Once I'm outside the door, Ms Benewood comes out and thanks the prefect for bringing me. Alison, or Amelie – whoever – shoots me a snide look as she walks off.

'Come in,' says Ms Benewood.

As I step into her office, I'm not even scared. What are they going to tell me off for? Kissing Tom outside school? There's hundreds of couples every year who kiss at school. Where else are we supposed to do it? It's not like I have my own place I can bring him home to every evening – most of the time that we get to see each other is on school grounds.

Ms Benewood clears her throat.

'Chloe, I think you already know why you're here. Sending school emails like that is completely unacceptable.'

*Emails?*

I look to see if she's laughing, but her face is stony.

For the first time, there's a stir of unease in my stomach.

116

# CHAPTER 25

# *Amber*

Monday morning, I reach the gym half an hour before registration. The air has a damp chill that sinks through my bones as I step into the warm entrance.

My head is buzzing with all the images I've looked at online over the past few days, trying to make sense of them. Ren. Ansh. Jerome. Last night, Seb had gone round to a mate's house, and he'd left WhatsApp web open on his laptop.

I didn't mean to read his group chat, I honestly didn't. But somehow within minutes, I'd opened the conversation and read something that made my throat turn dry.

In between the GIFs and in-jokes, there was a line from his mate Bill saying Jerome and Chloe got together at Tom's party.

There's been a weird, queasy feeling in my stomach ever since.

Maybe *Jerome* is the guy Seb saw with Chloe after the party – maybe *he* is the one who assaulted her. Maybe I'm not just being crazy. Maybe Ren really has been framed, and Jerome assaulted those girls.

My mind is working so fast that I don't even notice I've changed into my gym clothes. I absently make my way over to the equipment room, but there's a man standing there, blocking the entrance. I try to walk past, but he puts his hand out in front of me.

'Can't go in, I'm afraid. There's a class going on.'

I try to peer past him into the window, craning my neck. 'Um, yeah – I'm in that class.'

His eyes flick to the school eagle crest on my PE jumper. 'No high-schoolers,' he grunts.

No 'high-schoolers'? *Seriously?*

But I don't say anything back. I just mutter 'sorry' and look at the floor.

I'm not going to be able to speak to Ansh today to find out anything more about Ren. It's a completely wasted day. I'm going to go to school, sit by myself all lunch, then go back to lessons, and in the afternoon, sit bored out of my mind for the entire day.

Looking outside from the leisure centre entrance, I'm so close to the window pane, my nose is almost pressed up against the glass. Staring out at the gym car park, I can almost make out the school field. Though of course, at this time, it's empty. My eyes settle on a guy with a shock of dark hair, leaning against the back wall, a gym bag slung over one shoulder.

My heart gives a little lurch. *Is it Ren?*

But then I focus on him, and the fizzy feeling inside me settles. His eyes flick vaguely in my direction, and my mouth drops open. It may not be Ren, but it's the next best thing: Ansh.

I fling open the door to the gym and practically run towards him. As I get closer, he stands up a bit straighter, looking alarmed.

118

By the time I reach him, I'm red-faced and out of breath.

He blinks. 'Ren's sister? Amber, is it? Are you OK?'

But I can't speak; I'm bent forward clutching my chest.

Oh God, why am I so *unfit*?!

'Y-y-yes,' I gasp out in between breaths.

Ansh's eyebrows shoot up. There's a warm, prickling sensation in my cheeks. Now I'm here, I don't know what to say.

Oh God, *why* did I run over like that?

Ansh scrape s one of his trainers across the floor. There's an uncomfortably long silence.

'So, how's Ren?' he says.

My eyes widen – how does he know I've been watching Ren . . . But then I shake myself. Duh. He thinks I'm his sister.

'Oh, yeah, y'know, he's doing OK. Still a bit down about everything that happened.' I glance at Ansh, trying to gauge his reaction, but he's squinting into the distance.

'Yeah, I can imagine,' he says.

I tilt my head to one side. 'So, I mean, um, do you think he did it?'

Ansh looks at me sharply. 'What?'

'Well, it just seems like . . . I have a few—'

'I *know* he did it,' says Ansh.

'But how do you know?'

There's a long pause.

'People don't just lie about things like that,' he says eventually.

'But – when you posted that photo with Maisie—'

I suddenly stop talking, afraid of what I've just said. Ansh's face is scrunched up, and his eyebrows have descended to form a furrow below his hairline.

'Sorry, what?'

'Nothing. Nothing!' I step away, feeling my face flush. 'Anyway, um, I have to go . . .'

'Wait,' Ansh says, stepping forward, his voice quieter. 'Don't go looking for what he did.'

But I can barely hear him. My mind is ringing with the things that I've given away. That I stalked the picture Ansh posted of Jerome and Maisie. That I'm a complete and utter freak.

I back further away. 'AnywayI'vegottagobye!'

Ansh looks like he wants to say something else, but I don't let him. I turn on my heel and walk as quickly as I can back towards the school, almost tripping over my feet, I'm stumbling so fast.

I almost said about Jemma's date, the tagged photo, the video. I almost told Ansh that I'd stalked his Facebook and Ren's Instagram. And, oh God, I sent him a message. He must think I'm such a freak. But then again, he didn't mention it, did he? Maybe he hasn't been on Instagram yet. Oh God, maybe he's going to find my message now and think I'm even weirder.

The path starts to blur as I make my way back to the school field. Why do I always do this?

Why can't I, *for once*, act normally?

When I get back into school, I make a beeline for the nearest toilets, which happen to be the Year Nine's. I throw myself through the doors, go to the very last cubicle at the end, and bolt myself in.

Sitting down, I realize I've left my phone back up in my gym locker. So rather than refreshing Ren's Instagram page, I just sit there and stare at the back of the cubicle door, horrible thoughts circling my mind until the bell rings twenty minutes later.

# CHAPTER 26

# *Chloe*

It turns out, I'm not going to get a chance to speak to Louise at break. I haven't even made it to first period. I'm trailing along the back path, by myself, my scarf wound tightly around my neck, packed in my short, padded coat as the wind whips my hair across my lips.

I've been sent home. Suspended for five days.

Ms Benewood has called Mum and left a message. I'm dreading what she will say when I step through the door. The sick feeling in my stomach is growing worse and worse. Queasy, whirling, cramping. I feel like I'm going to hurl at any moment.

I stare at the stone ground in front of me, gnawing my lip. The walkway starts to blur before my eyes.

I just don't understand what's going on. First Louise freaking out, and now this.

Ms Benewood said I'd sent 'inappropriate photographs of Louise Bailey to the male students in my class'. I thought I was going to burst out laughing when she first said it. If the whole situation wasn't so unnerving, I would have done.

But as she was talking, my blood began to run cold. I remembered several months ago, when Louise was dating that guy Yousef, she asked my opinion on the photos she was going to send him. She sent me bikini photos over WhatsApp. And I helped her choose the best ones.

They're saved on my phone, but I've never sent on any of those photos, not to anyone. At least, I don't remember sending those messages.

But how would anyone else have gotten those photos?

I stop dead in the middle of the path. A chilling feeling grips my chest.

Am I losing it? How could I be doing these things and not even remembering?

My head starts to swim.

I know I've been feeling different recently. Spooked since the party . . . Do I even remember his name?

I shake my head, trying to get a grip on my thoughts.

No. I definitely didn't send those photos. I don't remember doing it.

*That doesn't mean you didn't send them. How drunk were you at the party?*

But they weren't in my sent emails, either. I opened up my school email on my phone to show Ms Benewood.

'Look. I promise I didn't send them!' I said, waving the screen under her nose.

But she just met my eye and said, in a level voice, 'I might not be on Snapchat or Instagram, but even *I* know you can delete sent emails, Chloe.'

122

My phone is vibrating. Slowly filling up with messages from Tom and people from school wanting to hear the gossip. I bet even more messages are swirling around that I can't see. Messages from people gossiping about me, sharing the photos of Louise. It's probably the talk of the entire school.

I feel a heat rising in my cheeks and – away from everyone, before I have to face Mum – I let a tear fall down my cheek.

I sniff into the navy sleeve of my school jumper, my stomach churning and churning.

Another tear leaks down my face.

Either this is one big giant prank, or there are bits of Tom's party I really don't remember.

# CHAPTER 27

## Amber

Later that morning, I'm sitting in chemistry, trying not to fall asleep as Ms Woodford drones on about the components of an atom. I'm swiping through Ren's recent locations, my brain buzzing with all the possible reasons he could have been set up, when my phone lights up with a message.

I'm so used to getting push notifications from various apps that it takes me a few seconds to realize it's a full-blown message, not just some reminder telling me to 'check back in'.

> **AnshMan** Sorry I missed your message earlier. How's your afternoon going?

It's sitting there, nestled between the status updates and 'you may have missed' messages, like it's just like any other notification, but it's not. This is a message someone sent to me – *only* me.

I read it almost instantly, but it takes a few moments to sink in.

Ansh messaged me back, after I behaved like a complete freak in the gym this morning and made out I was some kind of online stalker.

Why would he do that?

Slowly, I pick up my phone and stare at the keyboard.

I go to my notes app and start typing out a few different messages so he won't know how long it takes me to write something. Eventually I type back:

> **Amber0789** Good, thanks – trying not to fall asleep in chemistry ☺. How's yours?

He almost instantly sends a GIF of a cat sleeping on a keyboard. My mouth unwillingly lifts into a smile. I want to apologize now – send a long message saying sorry for being so weird this morning. I start typing one out in my notes, but then stop.

I think of the way Seb's phone dings almost constantly with hundreds of messages. How he just fires off a response without thinking about it. The way he never goes too deeply into things.

I swipe across to cat GIFs and send one of a kitten wearing comic glasses and a little hat, studying.

Ansh almost instantly sends back a crying-with-laughter emoji.

I tap on the message again, and a warm feeling radiates through my chest.

# CHAPTER 28

## *Chloe*

'No, Mum – I'm trying to tell you I *didn't* send those email s . . . Mum, stop – *please*! I didn't—'

I'm sitting at the kitchen table across from Mum, who has just found out about the suspension and is screaming at me at the top of her lungs.

'Just *wait* until your father hears about this!' She shakes her head in disbelief. 'Sending rude emails to boys! Taking naked photos of Louise? What is wrong with you?'

'Mum, please! You've got to believe me! I didn't send emails to any boys, or take photos of Louise.' Even as I say the words, I can feel a stirring in my gut.

*But did you send them? Can you be sure?*

Mum stabs at the printed-out piece of paper in front of her. It's a suspension letter Ms Benewood emailed over this afternoon. 'It says your name right here. C. MacNeil in the sent-email bit. It's even from *your* email address. You can see it at the top. Who else could have sent it?'

My head starts to thump. I honestly can't give her an answer. There's a dull ache behind my eyes. It's almost like there's a brass band in my head, pummelling my brow, drumming into my skull.

I put my head in my hands.

'I didn't do it, Mum. Why won't you believe me?' I whisper, tears pricking the back of my eyes.

Mum stops mid-rant. 'Why do you have to make my life so difficult? Why can't you be like the other girls who stay in and do their homework?'

'I'm doing well at school, I do my homew—'

She cuts me off. 'You're a tearaway! You're obsessed with drinking and going out. All you ever do is post hundreds of selfies with your boobs out! And now, *apparently*, take photos of your friends' boobs too!'

A hot feeling spreads over my cheeks.

'Why are you looking at my Instagram photos?!'

'*Everyone* can see your Instagram photos!' she shouts back. 'How do you think it looks for me, having such an embarrassment for a daughter?' Mum puts a hand on her forehead and sits down at the kitchen island. 'God, you've nearly given me a heart attack. Just go – I can't deal with you any more. I need to speak to your father.'

I open my mouth to say something – anything – but all of a sudden, I find I can't speak. A thump of pain in my head almost knocks me to the ground.

But I don't fall to the floor. I grip the chair, stand up, and walk to my room.

On the way up the stairs, I'm overcome by a sense of complete and utter defeat. My own mum doesn't believe me. But then again, I hardly even believe myself. Ms Benewood thinks I'm guilty. So does Louise, obviously. And probably everyone at school. They all think I got with Jerome, even though I can barely even remember his face.

But then again, do I really remember Joshua's face? Or even know that was his name for certain?

*You could have kissed Jerome. When you were smashed, at the party. Who's to know? It's the sort of thing you'd do, isn't it . . .*

And yet, it's not the sort of thing I've done. At least, not in the past. Maybe I did get with Jerome and forget. But the emails, sending all those boys photos of Louise – it just seems bizarre. I never log into my school emails unless we've had homework set. I don't even have them on my phone. And I wouldn't want to hurt Louise; she's one of my best friends.

I think back to the party. I remember how I behaved: desperate for attention, constantly looking over to where Tom was. I feel Joshua's lips on mine, or maybe Jerome's. I can feel a burning inside me, the jealousy I know I get when someone I like prefers someone else . . .

There's a weird, sick feeling in my stomach. Everything I've tried to suppress the last week is slowly coming back.

*WHORE.*

The fifty messages Sven sent to me that  morning before I blocked him. The lingering, unsettled feeling in the back of my mind that I couldn't quite put my finger on.

Am *I* the bitch? Did *I* do all this to Louise just for attention?

It feels like there's one person who would know. The same person who knew what I really was before.

In my bedroom, I open up Instagram on my phone and click

on Sven's page. He's still blocked, but my hand hovers over the three dots by the side of his name.

*Should I unblock him?*

My hand rests over the screen, but after a few seconds, I click off of the app. I need to speak to someone who actually knows me.

I message Tom, asking him to WhatsApp call me. After a couple of minutes of no response, I press his call icon.

The phone rings and rings. But he doesn't pick up.

I nibble on my lip. But it's Tom – it's fine. He's my best friend – I don't need to worry.

Pushing the stupid thoughts to the back of my mind, I type Tom's name into my Instagram to see the photos of us together.

I blink.

*Where is his page?*

I try typing his name a couple more times, but nothing comes up. There are hundreds of other Tom Taylors . . . but not *my* Tom – not his page.

I click through to my own photos. There are no comments from Tom. Not any more. Every single one has been deleted.

Has he *blocked* me?

My hands start to tremble. I feel like I'm overreacting, but I can't help myself. Gnawing my lip, I throw on my trainers and a hoody, grab a rucksack – where I stuff my phone, laptop, tablet, anything tech I can think of – and without even a backwards glance, I run down the stairs and out the front door, slamming it shut behind me.

# CHAPTER 29

# *Amber*

'He's not still doing it, is he, Maisie? *Oh-my-God*, he sounds obsessed!' A shrill voice echoes through the school corridor.

I'm walking back along the concourse at lunch, staring down at the emoji Ansh sent me on my phone, when I hear a girl from the year below shrieking with one of her friends.

My ears prick. Maisie Evans. *Maisie*. The first girl – the one whose house Ren supposedly turned up at – was a Maisie.

*Could it be . . .?*

I slow down and start pretending to look for something in my bag. Maisie and her friend get up and start walking towards the computer room, continuing their conversation in hushed tones.

I glance after them, and then back to my phone screen.

This is ridiculous, isn't it? I can't just follow them into the computer room. I haven't even seen her face, I don't know if this is the right Maisie . . . But then again, how many Maisies are there in the school? There's none in our year. One in the year above, I think. Then this Maisie Evans in the year below.

There's probably a one in three chance that this is *the* Maisie, that I've just stumbled on to something important, and I'm about to lose the most vital clue about Ren I've found so far.

I think about all the hours and hours I've spent staring at images of Ren, the location map, the dates I've tried to match up.

It could all end up being for nothing; I might never find out the truth.

Without thinking too much about what I'm doing, I make a U-turn and follow Maisie and her friend into the computer room. When I enter, they're sat huddled over two computers in one corner, heads together, gossiping. There's no one else in the room, so it's pretty easy to make out what they're saying.

Still, I sit fairly close – a few computers away – and then plug in my muted headphones so they don't think I'm listening.

I click open my biology homework task and hover my mouse over the folder. After several minutes of hushed conversation, my ears prickle.

'He hasn't stopped, y'know,' says Maisie, so quietly it's almost a whisper.

I glance over, but neither of them are paying attention to me. Her friend is staring at her with a pained expression.

'But you've blocked him, right? You told him to stop?'

'You know I have! Like a million times. I don't know what else I can do.'

'Go to the police.'

Maisie scoffs.

Her friend leans forward. 'No, seriously. Go to the police. They can warn him or something – they can sort him out.'

'No – he'll get bored eventually.'

'Has he got bored so far?'

I glance over, but this time, there's no chance of me being caught. Both girls don't even seem to realize there's anyone else in the room. Maisie is twisting her thumbs round and round in her palm.

'He will though. He's not a psychopath. He knows that I'm not interested.'

Her friend lets out a low sigh. 'It's messed-up that he thinks this is romantic.'

'I know!' says Maisie. 'He said he's going to send me a heart every day until I change my mind.'

'A *heart*?! As in, an actual *human* heart?' Maisie's friend's eyes are so wide that Maisie bursts out laughing.

'No, you idiot! Not an actual heart. Ew. A heart emoji. I got them every morning until I blocked him.'

'Oh-my-*God*!'

Her friend leans closer to Maisie, and I can only just lip-read her softly spoken words.

'Every girl in school is behind you, y'know. We all think he's a creep.'

My mouth turns dry. Every girl in school thinks Ren did it? Apart from me. I'm his *only* hope.

I'm staring so hard at Maisie and her friend that I don't even blink. At that moment, Maisie looks up and catches my eye. I feel my cheeks flush.

She clears her throat and inclines her head slightly to me. Her friend follows her gaze and then frowns.

'Let's head out,' she says.

I stare resolutely at the screen, clicking and pretending to type something for my biology homework as they walk out in silence.

As soon as they're both outside, they start hissing and whispering, glancing back at me through the doorframe.

My entire body feels like it is on fire.

Oh *God*.

*Why was I so bloody obvious?*

I want to get as low to the ground as possible and hide beneath the floorboards. I wish I could sink deeper and deeper. So deep, nobody could see me. No one would know I was there.

I could just sit there, hidden, forever.

At that moment, my phone dings again. Another message, from Ansh.

I tap it open. There's a GIF of a goose running towards another, bigger goose. It slips straight through the mud, and they both land on their back, squawking.

He's written, *Me, trying to teach people how to deadlift this afternoon*.

I stare at the message for a few moments.

I don't know why he's messaging me.

I don't mean that in a silly way. I mean I genuinely don't know why he's bothered to send me that GIF. No one else bothers to message me. Everyone else thinks I'm this freakish girl who sits at a computer by herself at lunch and stalks girls in the year below.

No one in my actual year thinks I'm worth speaking to.

I type out a crying-with-laughter emoji, even though I feel like actually crying.

Ansh almost instantly sends a beaming-face emoji back.

And then, even though it's the most pathetic thing in the world, I look at his message and actually do cry.

# CHAPTER 30

## *Chloe*

My rucksack is bumping against my lower back, the rain pelting against the fabric of my hoody, which I've stuffed my hair into. A bitingly cold gust of wind chills me to the bone, and my teeth start to chatter.

The bits of my hair that fall out either side of my face are wet, stringy, and starting to turn to natural frizz. I pull my sleeves over my fingertips and huddle my arms together, walking even faster.

I don't pay attention to where I'm going. My feet know the way.

As the path curves, I swallow hard. I'm beginning to feel actually scared.

*Did I email those photos of Louise to the boys in class? Did I get with Jerome?*

He could have mentioned he liked her. I could have got annoyed, seen the photos she sent me, and grasped the opportunity to humiliate her.

The phone clutched in my hand is splattered with rain. I try to unlock it, but the screen is too slippery. Even from the lock screen, I can see Tom hasn't responded.

The skin on my lip splits as I gnaw it, and I taste the metallic tang of blood.

I just need to find out what the hell's going on. The worst bit is not knowing. Whether someone like J, or Sven, is somehow setting me up . . . But then, they'd need those photos of Louise, and I don't know how that would be possible.

*Or maybe* . . . No – she wouldn't do that.

I stop walking.

*Could Louise have done this?*

I shake my head almost as soon as I think of it. No.

She does know the password to my school email address; she's logged on before to help me with homework. But why would she send out those photos of herself? There must be a better explanation.

I mean, I *did* drink a lot. I *could* have got with Jerome at Tom's party. But then, no one has mentioned it other than Louise. Particularly none of the guys. Gossip travels pretty fast, usually.

*None of this makes sense.*

My shoulders are heaving and falling, and I realize with a start that I've run all the way to Tom's house. I'm standing outside the large, beamed cottage. There's honeysuckle creeping up a lattice by the door, and ivy snaking along the aged brickwork. With a sniff and a shiver, I knock a few times on the door.

Tom's mum answers. She's a slim, plump-faced blond woman with just the beginnings of fine lines scattered across her kind eyes – piercingly blue like Tom's.

'Can I speak to Tom?' I say, breathless. My voice comes out as a croak.

Tom's mum peers closer. 'Chloe? Is that you?'

My hood is done up so tightly around my face that only my eyes are peeping out. I can feel tendrils of my hair bunching out either side of the fabric, and I try to smooth them down.

'Um, yes, it's me.'

Tom's mum waves me inside. 'Oh g osh! Silly me. I hardly recognized you in that hoody!'

She shouts for Tom, and he comes bounding down the stairs, grinning. I pull the hood off my face and try to shake out my hair – but I can feel it's a wet clump of half-formed frizz.

Tom laughs when he sees me.

'Raining was it?' he says, coming over to put his arms around me, but I duck out of his embrace.

'Why didn't you reply to my messages?' I say.

He shoots a look at his mum, who quietly slips out into the kitchen.

'What? Er, I was working out in the study – my phone's upstairs.'

I can feel my heart rate start to slow. So he wasn't ignoring me. But something's still wrong.

'Why did you delete all your Instagram comments on my photos, then?'

'Ah.' Tom's face has changed. He shoots a glance into the kitchen, where his mum is. 'I didn't really want to have to tell you, what with everything that happened before. I didn't want you to get the wrong end of the stick—'

He nods. 'Come upstairs. I'll show you.'

I pull off my trainers, feeling my damp socks clinging to my feet, and pad up the stairs behind him, my stomach tightening with every step.

# CHAPTER 31

# Amber

After school, I'm kneeling down by the bike rack, tucking one of my shoelaces that slipped out back into my shoe, when I see Ansh walking across the path, playing something on his phone, his sports bag slung over one shoulder.

I feel a jolt of surprise on seeing him again, even though I know he was working this morning, so it makes sense his shift would be ending about now.

I get up and walk over. When he sees me, he lifts up his hand and gives a little half-smile. I nod, not quite sure how to respond, and his face creases like I've done something hilarious.

'Did you see the gym picture I sent over?' he says.

I did. During last period, he sent an image of the packed gym with *busy afternoon* underneath, and I spent the last thirty minutes of class trying to work out how I should respond. I actually typed out three different replies in the notes app on my phone, but I couldn't decide which to send.

'Yeah,' I say, glancing at him. 'It was, um, cool.'

Ansh slips his phone into his pocket and falls into step with me. I catch his eye.

He shakes his head, smiling. 'I wish you wouldn't look at me like that,' he says.

'Like what?'

'Like I'm a monster who's come to terrorize the village children.'

It's such a weird thing to say that I pull a face at him, and he immediately grins.

'You're so weird,' I say without thinking, then immediately wish I hadn't. Who am I to say that? I'm the weirdest person in the world. *I literally turned up outside Ren's house.*

'*I'm* weird?!' He looks like I've just told him he's on fire when I'm the one with my head aflame.

'Well, not that weird,' I say quickly.

'*Not that weird,*' he repeats back, glancing at me with a funny expression.

'What?'

He shakes his head. 'No, no – it's nothing. Just . . .' He smiles. 'Just you.'

I don't really know what to say to that, so I keep walking and staring at the ground. After a couple of seconds, Ansh takes his phone back out and passes it to me.

'Have you seen this short film? It's been nominated for an Oscar.'

I take the screen dutifully and start watching the little clip. As I glance up, I see Ansh is watching for my reaction. Suddenly he nods.

'There's a great bit here, where the kid tricks the other one. Look—'

He leans in closer to me, pointing at the screen. As he tilts his head down to mine, I suddenly become aware of how hot my body feels – how bizarre this whole conversation is.

Why would Ansh even *bother* to speak to me again?

As he stands there, I can't help thinking of all the times I've looked at his social media profiles, searching for images of Ren. Just by skimming them, I know every holiday he's had in the last three years. I even know what his mum looks like after seeing that photo he posted of her by the Aga at Christmas brandishing the turkey.

Ansh's shoulders shake beside me. 'This bit is great,' he says, his eyes on the screen in my palm.

But I can't concentrate on what he's saying. My mind is buzzing with everything I know about him. Whether that's normal. Whether I'm normal. Or whether I'm a complete and utter—

'Do you ever look at people's families on Instagram?' my mouth says before my brain has a chance to register the question and stop me.

Ansh frowns. 'Huh? Look at people's families on Instagram? Uh, I don't—' He's looking at me now, not the screen, and his brow is knitted. 'Why'd you ask?'

'Oh! Nothing – I just . . . I don't know. I—'

He reaches over to take his phone back, and I jerk away from him so abruptly, it jumps out of my hands, clattering to the pavement. Quickly, I duck down and snatch the phone back, but now it's locked, and the video has stopped playing.

'I'm so sorry – I just dropped it . . . I didn't mean to—'

'Nah, don't worry about it. It's fine,' says Ansh, wiping a bit of dirt off of his screen once I pass it back to him. But his eyes are still narrowed as he slips the phone back into his pocket.

Then he focuses on my face. 'Why are you so red?'

# CHAPTER 32

## *Chloe*

The photos open on Tom's laptop in his bedroom are selfies of girls posing in bikinis. Not just one, but hundreds and hundreds of different women. Pouting, pushing their boobs out, winking seductively at the camera.

I stare, dumbfounded, as he clicks through them – his ears turning pink.

'This is why I deleted my Instagram,' he says. 'I didn't want to have to show you.'

My eyes are flitting across the screen as though searching for answers.

'I don't understand,' I say, wincing at the thump in my head. 'Why do you have so many photos of girls in bikinis?'

'They were sent to me – hundreds of them. I started getting them a few days ago.'

'From who?'

Tom frowns. 'I don't know. Probably a spambot. I just didn't want you to see them on my phone . . . Look.' Tom spins the laptop towards me. 'At first, I started blocking these girls, thinking they were a prank, but they kept coming. I got Rishaan to track the IP addresses of each of the accounts though, and they all come from the same place. They couldn't even be bothered to use a proxy.'

Tom sees my face and sighs. 'I'm sorry. It's so messed-up.'

I look down at my hands and see my fingers are shaking slightly.

Tom follows my gaze.

'Hey, it's OK.' He comes over and wraps his arms around my shoulders. 'It's fine – I'll run a virus scanner and reinstate my account once it's cleaned up.'

But there's a tightness in my throat. It's like this madness is seeping into every part of my life. How can I stop these things from happening?

Is it Louise? Or Sven? J, even? Who at school would want to do something like this?

It feels humiliating that someone has the power to do this to me. I don't want to tell anyone, I just want to make them stop.

I sniff hard and shake Tom's arms off me.

'It's just a spambot, no big deal,' he says.

My bottom lip starts to quiver. 'It's not just that. I think . . . I think whoever did this has sent messages to Louise too, or the other people at school. Everyone thinks I got with Jerome. And at school – today I got called into Ms Benewood's office and was accused of sending topless photos of Louise that have been going around class from my email address. I've been suspended for five days.'

Tom steps back. His face has changed slightly. 'You *what*?'

My eyes widen. 'I didn't send them. At least I don't

remember . . . I don't know what's going on!' I say, and tears spill down my cheeks.

***

An hour later, after finishing two cups of tea, Tom is sitting at the edge of his bed a little way across from me, elbows resting forward on his thighs, staring into the mug in his hands.

He frowns. 'So you honestly didn't get with Jerome at the party? Or send those pictures?'

For a second, I open my mouth and tilt my head to one side, ready to admit the truth: *I don't know – I can't remember.* But then I look up and see his jaw is set. No, I don't want to lose Tom again. I can't deal with that – not now.

'No. I . . . Yes, I'm sure I didn't.'

Tom's lip curls. 'Sure?'

'Definitely sure! I wouldn't have done something like that.'
*You might have . . .*

Tom looks at me for a few seconds and then sighs. 'Fine. If you genuinely didn't do it—'

'I didn't. I promise!'

'Well, yeah, sure. If you actually didn't, then something's seriously going on, and we need to sort it.'

I gnaw the inside of my cheek. 'But how? We can hardly go to the police and say someone is spreading rumours about me, sending nudes from my emails, pretending to be me?'

Tom raises one eyebrow. 'Well actually, we can – if you have proof. It's not just school stuff – this is identity theft. There's no way this is legal. I don't know the law that well, but it'll fall under something. Harassment – stalking, maybe.'

I'm beginning to feel a glimmer of hope. Maybe we can go to the police and get them to make this stop. Tom's right – it can't be legal to completely wreck someone's life like this.

*But what if there's not someone else doing this to you? What if you've done it all yourself . . .*

I shake my head as Tom goes on. 'They'll have ways of looking into this. Tracking what people have done. It's all there, online. They'll be able to find evidence.'

'What if there's no proof,' I say before I can stop myself.

Tom's face hardens. 'Why would there be no—'

'No, no! Sorry, that's stupid. You're right – they'll be able to find something. Definitely.'

'Well, yeah, if someone's behind this, they will.' Tom looks right at me.

Moving across the bed, I wrap my arms around him and rest my head on his shoulder, feeling the warmth of his skin beneath his T-shirt, wishing this would all disappear.

# CHAPTER 33

## *Amber*

When I get in from school, I don't say hello to Mum, Dad or Seb before going up to my room and slamming the door shut. It's like my mind is screaming silently. I can feel the horror of what I said to Ansh. Him knowing I've looked at his Instagram, thinking I'm a sad, lonely stalker with no friends.

I force my face down into my soft duvet and let out a wail, muffled, so no one downstairs can hear. It's like my thoughts are working on overdrive. I can't make them stop; my whole body is flushing hot.

I need something to relax me. I need to feel better.

Frantically I pull out my phone and click through Ren's social media pages. But there's nothing new to distract me. I try a few of his friends' Instagram profiles, but I've seen them all.

Nothing.

Nothing.

Nothing.

*Wait a minute . . .*

My eyes fall on a new image posted from one of the guys he plays football with. The image is tiny, and Ren is way, way in the back – you can only just about make out his face – but I instantly dash to my laptop and flip it open.

Biting my lip so hard it hurts, I screenshot the image on my phone, Facebook Messenger it to myself, and within seconds, I've downloaded it onto my laptop and added it to my slideshow.

I feel weirdly calm as I watch the images flick from one to another. But the more I watch them, the less it works, the more my back stiffens.

I catch sight of my reflection in the mirror. My eyes are slightly bloodshot from staring at the screen, and I have a huge pimple beneath my lip, which is so big, it almost looks like a second chin. Looking away, I focus on the dark wall of my room, realizing I never bothered to turn the light on when I came in.

As I look away from the screen, I feel a bit weird. To be honest, ever since I started trying to find out about whether Ren has been set up by Jerome, I've felt a bit weird.

It's like . . . I shouldn't be doing this.

No, not just that. It's like I'm a freak.

I think again of my stupid comment to Ansh, and my eyes burn with tears of humiliation.

He'll think I'm a freak, which I am. He'll think I'm this obsessed stalker, which I also am.

I grimace at my black reflection in my phone screen. On the laptop, my tabs from last night are still open, and each one of them is on one of Ren's social media profiles.

Rhythmically, I click through them, in the same order I always do. Instagram main photos. Then tagged photos. Then the photos of his close friends. Their tagged photos. Then, once I'm sure there are no new posts, onto Twitter.

Next: the leisure centre. Their blog, Facebook page, any updates.

And finally I check his Facebook. He doesn't use his Facebook that much; it hasn't been updated in two months, which is why I always check it last.

Idly, I click refresh on his page.

A message pops up: *One new update.*

My heart actually skips a beat.

An update? But he hasn't posted in the whole two months I've been watching his page.

I almost headbutt the screen, I lean forward so quickly to click on it. It's a status post – a very long block of text.

Christ. And he's mentioned the gym. This could tell me everything.

I grip the laptop so hard, it almost topples over my lap as I crane my neck to read it. I skim the post in double-quick time. He's talking about his life, the last few months, how grateful he is to the people who actually believe him, how betrayed he feels, but how, despite everything, he's staying strong and not going to let 'pathetic liars' get him down.

For the next ten minutes, I reread Ren's words until they start to blur into one black smudge on the screen.

A girl from school, Tabetha, has commented underneath.

**Tabetha Melton** *Pathetic?* ***@IuliaAlexe*** *have you seen this? You're the only one who's lying, mate.*

In response, Iulia has just written one line:

**IuliaAlexe** *This is too pathetic to respond to. We both know what you did to me.*

I click on Iulia's profile. Is she the third girl?

She's the other trainee at the gym, the one with wavy, thick red hair. The one that helped me when I got stuck on the exercise bike. Who said hi to me at the garden centre.

My eyes dart across the screen.

The one who is down on the rota to open up the gym tomorrow.

# CHAPTER 34

# Chloe

Tom's mum lets us borrow the car so he can drive me to the police station. We don't tell her where we're going – we just say we 'fancy a drive', as I can't bear the thought of explaining the situation to even more people.

We drive in silence the whole way there, Tom clutching the steering wheel and staring ahead. I can't work out what he's thinking: whether he believes that I didn't do any of it; or whether he secretly thinks (as even I do) that I might have.

Sitting in the passenger seat, it feels like every cell of my body is made of glass, and I could shatter at any moment.

'This is it,' says Tom, pulling the car up at the side of the road and squinting at his phone. 'Yeah, this is the pin location. We're here.'

The chill of the cool night air is seeping through the glass car windows. I shudder, and he glances over at me.

'You OK?'

The tall building has *Ferrington Town Constabulary* written on a plaque to the right of the double wooden doors.

'Mm-hmm,' I mumble.

Tom leaves the car before I have time to hesitate. Gnawing the inside of my cheek, I hurriedly follow him inside.

There's just one police officer sitting at the front desk, grinning and shouting something over his shoulder to one of his mates. When he sees us, he doesn't stop laughing. In fact, he turns around and shouts something else.

We stand there silently for a moment before I clear my throat.

The round, fat-faced police officer glances at me with a grin.

'Just a minute, darling,' he says, and he gets up to go over to the officer behind him.

Tom reaches over and takes my hand. '*You OK?*' he mouths. I nod.

There's a chill in the grey walls of the station, which is making me shiver. I pull the sleeves of my hoody over my hands and rub them together, fabric-to-fabric, to try to warm myself up.

After what seems like forever, the police officer returns.

'Sorry about that,' he wheezes, not sounding sorry at all. He sits down heavily on the other side of the desk. 'What can I do for you two?'

Tom takes out his phone and opens his mouth, but I don't want him to say it for me. I take a deep breath.

'I'd like to file a police report. I think I'm being . . . well, I *am* being . . . um, harassed. Online.'

'And she's a victim of identity theft,' adds Tom.

'Harassed?' says the officer, his eyebrows shooting up. 'And identity theft?'

'Yes. Well I think so,' I say.

I glance over at Tom, who nods encouragingly.

Slowly, I tell the police officer everything. As I speak, Tom points to screenshots, emails and notes we've collected on his phone. The police officer doesn't take any notes. He eyes both of us with a bored look. After a couple of minutes, he speaks.

'Miss – what was it? Mac . . .?'

'MacNeil.' My voice is oddly quiet.

'Miss MacNeil.' He stands up and begins to walk across the room. 'Come through here, please. I'll need to ask you a few questions.'

He nods to indicate that Tom can accompany me, and we follow him into a bare side room with a table and three cheap plastic chairs. He pulls one out and sits down, indicating for us to do likewise.

'Would you like a cup of tea?' he says.

I shake my head.

He leans back slowly in his chair, raises his eyebrows at me, and sighs.

'None of what you've just described to me is a crime.'

I glance at Tom, whose cheeks are turning pink.

I raise my eyebrows. 'None of it?'

The police officer shakes his head. 'Sadly, no.'

'What about impersonating me? Contacting people I know?'

The police officer's eyes are lolling around, glancing at the walls.

'Look. Pretending to be someone – for a bit, on social media – just isn't a crime.' There's starting to be an edge to his voice. 'And do you have any evidence of who is behind it?'

A chilled feeling rises in my throat. 'No, but you can . . . look at people's phones. For evidence.'

The police officer bites his lip, apparently to stop himself laughing. 'We can't do that without a warrant. And we don't have any evidence to justify that kind of intrusion into people's privacy.'

I can feel the familiar stirring in my stomach returning.

'What about the harassment?' I say suddenly, nodding to my phone. 'Tom got hundreds of requests from naked girls on his Instagram.'

The police officer looks like he is trying not to laugh. He shakes his head at Tom and turns to me. 'Have you ever felt scared for your life?' he says.

There's a pause. I think back to the fear I felt looking at my phone. The crazy, out-of-control feeling of not knowing what's happening.

*Scared for my life?*

'No.'

'Did any of these people ever physically threaten you?'

'Um, no—'

The police officer presses on, seeming to enjoy this.

'Have you ever been sexually intimate with the guy you suspect is behind this?'

My eyebrows shoot up.

'What? No! I don't even know—' But even as I say it, I can feel my cheeks inflaming.

The police officer takes a sip of his tea and leans forward. 'Now, how old is Louise? And what exactly do the pictures that were sent round of her show?'

An icy chill trickles down my spine. 'How *old* is Louise?' I whisper.

'Yes,' he says. 'If she's under eighteen, and the image is sexual in nature, then the person who sent that is breaking the law.' He puts down his pen. 'It is illegal to make, distribute, possess or show any indecent images of anyone aged under eighteen, even if the image was created with the supposed consent of that young person.'

My mouth drops open. Why on earth did I come here? Those images were from my email address – I'm going to end up *in prison* . . .

The police officer misinterprets my silence and sighs. 'I'm not trying to upset you. I'm just asking routine questions that make it possible for me to file a report. I can speak to your school if you like, to find out more.'

The thought of people at school looking into who actually sent those messages, knowing for certain whether it was me, makes me feel like I'm *really* going to throw up.

'No! No—' My voice cracks. 'It's fine. I'll just keep an, um, record.'

'Yes. And if you receive any physically threatening messages, let me know.'

'I will – I will,' I mumble.

The police officer stands up, pushing back his chair, and claps his hands together.

'Right, then. There you go.'

He smiles broadly, and all the tension from before comes pulsing back.

# CHAPTER 35

# Amber

The next morning, I don't even notice the icy chill of the air as I walk towards the leisure centre. Or the fact that my eyes are stinging, head is thumping, from lack of sleep. It's just after 6.30 a.m., and I stayed up until 2 a.m. last night trying to work out how I'm going to get Iulia to tell me what happened.

I mean, I can hardly just rock up and ask her what she thinks of Ren, can I? I've got to do something cleverer. I've got to *think*. But my brain is thick like treacle. And there's this aching crick in my neck from staring at all those screens that I can't shake.

I huddle down lower into my coat and refresh my Snap Map page a few times, though Ren is stubbornly offline. Stepping into the leisure centre, it takes me under a minute to rush to the changing room and get into my PE outfit.

Pretty soon I'm standing by the running machine, with Iulia perched the other side of the room. I keep glancing at her, and after a while, she catches my eye. I quickly put my head down – but she's already making a beeline for me.

I jab the buttons on the pad at random. There's a bleep from the machine, which makes me jump.

'Hey,' says Iulia in a soft, light tone, her red hair bouncing either side of her round face. 'Do you need any help with your fitness routine?'

'Um . . .' I don't know what to say. I'm so flustered, I can barely answer.

Iulia takes my lack of response as a yes.

She smiles. 'Here, let me talk you through our standard cardio workouts.'

She leans over and then starts explaining various exercise patterns. As she talks, I'm thinking about all the lines I rehearsed last night. I was going to start by asking how her morning was going, then say, 'Do you miss working with Ren?' Then gently ask what she meant, and soon she'd reveal what happened between them. Maybe even explain what she meant by her comment, *We both know what you did to me.*

'And that's it!' says Iulia, standing proudly back. 'Sound good? Let me know if you need any more help!'

She smiles, and then takes a step away. I'm just staring at her, my mouth hanging open.

This isn't what was meant to happen.

Oh God, now is my chance. My only chance. I've got to think of something – quick!

'Do you . . . D-do you know Ren Moore?'

Iulia is already halfway across the gym, and at the mention of Ren's name, her sunny face jerks into a frown. 'Ren? Why do you ask?'

I blink.

*Why do I ask?* How on earth do I answer that?

158

'Oh, I just . . . I don't know. I—'

My cheeks aren't just prickling now. They are completely aflame – and it feels like every hair on my body is getting singed.

Iulia is still frowning. Rather than walking away though, she takes a step forward.

Oh God, think of *something*. Quick!

'He's, um . . . He's . . . asked me out.'

*Where did that come from?*

My heart is thudding harder than ever, and I can't even meet Iulia's eye to gauge her reaction.

My voice comes out garbled. 'AndyouusedtoworkwithhimsoI wonderedwhatyouthought.'

Oh God. This is cringe. She is never, ever going to believe that Ren wanted to go on a date with me. I can't believe I said that.

*I AM SO STUPID!*

There's a tickle of long hair across my shoulders. When I look up, Iulia is standing dangerously close. But she's not frowning any more, her eyes are wide, and she looks like she wants to hug me.

'Have you been yet?'

'Um, what?' I say, unable to meet her eye.

'Have you been on any dates with him yet?'

'Er, no. Not yet.'

She purses her lips, leaning forward. Her pale grey eyes are so close to mine that I can't fully focus.

'Good,' she hisses. 'Don't.'

# CHAPTER 36

## *Chloe*

Mum still isn't speaking to me. By not speaking, I mean she shouts at me, screams things in my direction about 'tearaway teenagers' occasionally, but rolls her eyes every time I try to speak to her in a normal voice. This morning, she studiously ignored me while I ate breakfast and washed up our dishes, before getting on the phone to one of her horrible friends and shouting from the other room about how I've been suspended and what a 'nightmare' I am to live with.

Seriously, I don't even have the energy to fight her any more. If she doesn't want to believe me, fine. If Ms Benewood won't believe me either, then that's her problem, not mine.

I stare at my face in the mirror. I got up, showered, and did my make-up as usual. I even almost put on my school shirt this morning before I realized with a sinking feeling that I won't be going to school until next week.

I glance at my phone. Louise still hasn't messaged me. I typed out a long message to her last night explaining everything: how

I don't remember sending those emails; how I'm sorry; how we went to the police. But then I deleted it, remembering what happened the last time I sent a needy message to someone.

She'd probably show it to everyone at school, and it just makes me sound like some crazed, unhinged woman.

The police officer was right. There isn't any evidence. It also doesn't make sense how someone I don't know could know so much about my life to hurt me in this way. It might not even be someone I know.

It could be . . . *anyone*.

Who have I pissed off so much they would want to hack into my accounts?

I feel like everything in my life has become uncertain. It's not just what's happened – it's *me*. Usually Louise giving me the silent treatment wouldn't even bother me. I'd spend time chatting to Rachel and Ameerah. Get them on side. Then I'd be even louder and flirtier than usual with the guys in the class, making her want to come over.

But even if I was in school right now, I know I couldn't do that. It's like I'm numb.

I look down at my thumb and pick at a hangnail. It tears, and a few blobs of red trickle down onto my palm.

*What am I doing?*

Sliding my phone into my lap, I send a single WhatsApp message to Louise.

**Chloe** We need to talk.

***

162

We arrange to meet by the cafe in the high street after school. For some reason, I can't stop plucking at the hem of my loose jumper. The cold air is making my teeth tremble, and I'm just wearing jeans and trainers. I haven't bothered putting any make-up on, so I feel like half my face has been wiped away. I stare at the floor. It doesn't matter; it's fine.

When I look up, I see Louise coming towards me, and my body jolts. It's not just Louise. She's bought the whole gang. Ameerah, Rachel.

My bare face makes me want to hide.

Louise lets out a low sigh, her cat-like eyes narrowing. 'Whatever you have to say to me, you can say in front of everyone.'

I lift my chin up. Take a deep breath.

'OK – I know what's happened to you, and I'm so sorry about that.' It takes all my concentration to stop my voice trembling. 'But I don't lie—'

*How can you say that? You don't know you didn't get with Jerome.*

'I *didn't* get with Jerome. I've been with Tom most of the year, and besides, I would never betray a friend's trust like that. And I never sent those photos. Do you really think I'd do something like that?'

The reaction isn't quite what I was expecting. On any other day, the girls would be throwing Louise filthy looks, or at least looking unsure.

Instead, Rachel lets out a sigh, and Ameerah rolls her eyes.

'Oh pur-lease give it a rest,' says Louise with a snort. 'We all know the truth. We've seen it.'

'What have you seen? Have you even spoken to Jerome?'

Louise shrugs. 'Of course I have.'

'*And?*'

'He denies it too. Well done – you've got him to stick to a consistent story.'

'But you have no proof – it's a bloody rumour that you know isn't true!'

Ameerah's cheeks have developed two pale spots of pink while we've been talking. But now, she's tapping on her phone and shoves the screen under my nose.

'Is this enough proof for you?'

On the phone, there's a screenshot of an Instagram conversation between me and someone else. When I peer closer, I can see the familiar small icon of my profile picture, along with the name *Jerome Femi*.

> **Chlo03** Last night was amazing, thank you so much.

> **Jerome_F** I had an amazing time, but don't tell Louise. She'll be pissed.

And then there's me sending a zipped-mouth emoji.

It's so ridiculous that I almost burst out laughing.

'These messages are so fake. Do you really think I'd say something like that?'

'A girl from Jerome's school sent them to me. She thought I should know,' says Louise, lifting her chin.

'But which girl? Did you check her account? Did she have

164

any mutual friends? It's probably not even a real account! Someone's probably made up that message. Cut it together in photoshop.'

But I can see I'm losing them. The girls don't look irritated any more. Their faces are widening with a mixture of horror and pity.

'Seriously, I'm not . . . It sounds ridiculous, but—' I splutter.

Louise shakes her head.

'Stop, Chloe,' she says quietly. 'You're embarrassing yourself.'

# CHAPTER 37

# Amber

At lunch, all the kids in the younger years are sitting in groups around me chatting, while I sit on a bench by myself and eat my sandwiches. My brain is still whirring from what Iulia said to me at the gym this morning.

I can vividly imagine everything she told me in hushed whispered tones. Her starting personal training at the gym for the first time, meeting Ren and instantly hitting it off. Why wouldn't they? He's so nice, with his easy smile. And when he lifts his arm up, you can see the shadow of muscle running beneath his T-shirt.

I picture Iulia and Ren getting closer as they worked together each day. Them giggling on walks home; his eyes sparkling in the twilight. When it gets late, them grabbing a hot chocolate before the coffee shop closes; him walking her home, wrapping his arm around her shoulder.

She doesn't believe this is really happening, that he likes her too. Against the outline of the moonlight, he leans down to kiss her . . .

But that's where my fantasy stops.

I can't imagine the rest of what she told me. Him calling her a slut, making her cry. The constant calls and messages. Him turning up at her house – her father going out and shouting at him to go away.

I blink several times in the direction of the gym.

If she'd told me this about anyone else, I would never want to speak to them again. But there's something about her story that unnerves me, and not because of Ren.

Just . . . something doesn't feel *right*.

I tap open Ren's Instagram page instinctively. There are loads of girls commenting on his pictures, probably hundreds in total. Why would he want to behave like that to Iulia? Why would he need to, when so many girls adore him?

The dates on Jemma's story also don't quite add up. When I overheard Maisie in that computer room, I don't actually even know if she was the right Maisie, or if she was talking about Jerome instead. But Iulia's story is the one that makes me think. And at the start of the year too. I didn't get the exact date out of her, but she said this all happened when they began their course in September. It just seems so wrong.

There's a peal of laughter from a group of kids nearby, but I tune it out. I'm probably just making excuses for Ren. I don't know him – not really. How do I know what he's capable of? Everyone else is probably right, and I've just been duped. Maybe when he smiled, he was just trying to manipulate me, make me become one of his girls like Jemma, Maisie and Iulia.

I'm scrolling through Ren's Instagram feed aimlessly, flicking through the September dates. I have all his pictures memorized; I know I'm not going to find anything. When Iulia said 'September', I almost put my head in my hands right there because I know there are no tagged photos then. Only a few snaps of him and his friends, and one photo of him lifting weights in the mirror topless.

I sigh.

On autopilot, I click through to a few of his close friends. I end up on Ansh's Instagram page, skimming through September, when I find my eye caught by a photo posted on 2 September. It's a photo I know well because it has Ren in it, but it's not one I've ever paid attention to before – he's at the back, and you can't even really make out his face. Ansh, Ren, Iulia and a clutch of the other trainee personal instructors are lined up against the backdrop of the gym, grinning at the camera.

*First-year trainees!* he's written in the caption, with a flexing-bicep emoji and the hashtag *#firstdayfirstlifts*.

I squint at the screen. I'm sure college started in September. That's when Iulia will have first seen Ren in the gym.

I click through to the local college and start reading all their course details. Soon I find their PT one and skip to the page about placements.

*The first month of study will involve classroom-based work. Physical placements and assessments in gyms for first- and second-year PTs will take place in the first term, which runs from October until mid-December.*

I tap at the screen. Ren wears the same uniform and does the same course as Ansh and Iulia. If the course didn't start until October, then they wouldn't have met as personal trainers in September. And, as far as I can see, there would have been no reason for him or Iulia to start doing their placements early.

I stare at the screen for a full minute, while a group of Year Seven girls run past, giggling. This is getting ridiculous. I need to find out whether any of these girls have got the wrong guy. What more can I do? I'm already looking at every profile I can find online. I've spoken to Ansh, Iulia . . .

I clutch my head in my hands and tap on Ren's most recent Instagram story. I only look at his stories every other day, so he doesn't somehow find out how often I look at his profile. They're not useful, anyway – just usually clips of him working out.

This one is the same – images of him tensing in the mirror, smiling at the screen. But in the mirror reflection, I can see WhatsApp messages flashing across his screen.

I bite my lip. Wait a minute . . . There *is* a way to find out. To really know the truth.

I could message him.

Tapping open WhatsApp, I type in *Ren Moore*, and his saved contact immediately comes up. Swallowing a dry lump in my throat, I type *Hey* and then click send before I have a chance to think about what I'm doing.

Then I stare at my message. Delivered but unread. Two grey ticks.

And I sit there for the rest of lunch, closing and reopening the chat, waiting for him to see it.

# CHAPTER 38

## Chloe

Later that afternoon, I'm crouched over the laptop in my room, wrapped up tightly in a duvet cocoon, staring down at the bright blue screen with the lights off and curtains drawn.

I feel like I'm unravelling.

I've spent all afternoon sitting in this one spot, scrolling numbly through every Instagram feed I can think of. Mine. Louise's. Tom's. Jerome's. I'm scrolling through the photos from the party, skimming the tags for names beginning with *J*, but he's not coming up. I can't find his face anywhere.

I'm not even sure what I'm looking for. Some kind of hint as to who has done this?

I've also been reading about it online. Cyberstalking. That's what it's called when someone starts impersonating you or hacking your accounts online.

There's a freshly formed scab on my thumb, which I nibble away at so it spurts fresh globs of blood.

From what I've read about UK law on stalking, the accused's

behaviour must cause the victim 'serious alarm or distress that has a substantial adverse effect on their usual day-to-day activities'.

I think back to the police officer saying there wasn't enough evidence to look into it. He was bloody wrong. It *is* a crime.

A hot-water bottle is wound so tightly in my duvet that sweat beads on my brow. The beginnings of a heat rash prickle my forearm, but I ignore it.

How can I *prove* this is happening to me?

Mum. The teachers. Louise. Everyone at school. No one believes me. I don't even know who's doing this. There's absolutely no proof of anything.

*And there's no way to find out.*

If only there was some way I could take a look at the phone of whoever is doing this or get into their computer. I would know what is going on for sure. Then the police would have to do something. At the very least, the school, Mum and Louise would have to believe me.

My eyes feel scratchy and tired as I stare at the monitor. On the bed, my phone lights up with a few messages from Tom, but I let them flicker across the screen.

I don't want to speak to anyone.

I think back to the moment at the party that I've pushed to the back of my mind. J's hot, thick hands running over my body. The cold feeling of helplessness in my stomach. But I didn't know J. He didn't know me. He just wanted the power over me, but not *me* really; he didn't care that much. He barely even looked at me. To him, I could have been any girl.

As I'm clicking through my own page, I see the photo I posted of me and Tom. This is exactly when it all started happening, isn't it – when I uploaded this picture. The person who did this didn't assault me, blind drunk, at a party. The person who did this knows more about me than J ever did; he actually *cared* about seeing this photo of me and Tom. It can't have been J. It must be someone who saw this photo.

I scroll down to the comments. I blocked Sven's Instagram page, but his latest comment is still there, etched below the line.

**Sven_247** *Who is he?*

Hovering over Sven's Instagram page, I click the three-dots icon and, with trembling fingers, select *Unblock this user*.

My stomach flutters as his page pops up. Immediately I can see all his photos again.

I'm surprised by how good-looking he is. In my mind, he had become some kind of creep, but his page is filled with pictures of his broad, handsome smile. Photos with friends, ones of him on holiday or by the beach. For a second, I'm caught by a black and white image of him tensing with rippling muscles, the hollows of his dark cheekbones strikingly defined.

In the comments, there are loads of messages from girls. He's responded to a few of them with winks and kissing-face emojis. Who are these girls? Would he really cyberstalk me when he gets so much attention already?

I click through to a couple of the girls' profiles. Weird. They each have just one or two photos and only follow Sven.

Are these . . . *fake accounts?*

They must be. No one has an Instagram account and only follows one person.

The queasy feeling is slowly returning in my stomach. If he

has set these girls' profiles up, then what else could he have done? He was annoyed, wasn't he, when I got back with Tom . . .

But he wasn't just annoyed. He was livid.

My fingertips fidget in front of the screen. For the first time, I'm beginning to feel sure. It must be him behind this. It all makes sense. He got annoyed, wanted to sabotage my life.

But how would he know about Jerome?

How would he have those photos of Louise?

Pushing the doubt to the back of my mind, I swipe across into my DMs. I'm going to put an end to this. I'm going to make him confess. I lick my dry lips and click on Sven's conversation. There are hundreds of unanswered messages.

I don't know him at all – but also, he doesn't know me. And two can play at this game.

> **Chlo03** OMG SO weird. My Instagram seems to have deactivated loads of accounts, but yours is back now. Only just seen these messages. I thought you had ghosted me! Haha. How are you? How have you been?!

As I predicted, his icon lights up to show he's online almost instantly.

I click out of the app; I can't bear to wait for his reply.

Will this even work?

I drum my fingers against the base of my laptop.

It takes longer than I was expecting – about three minutes – but finally my phone lights up with a new message. Then three.

**Sven_247** Your phone deleted me? You serious? How did that happen?

**Sven_247** . . .

**Sven_247** Weird. I'm good anyway, I guess. How about you?

**Chlo03** I'm good. I missed speaking to you. I was thinking, we should meet up. We chatted for so long, it seems weird we never got to meet in person!

This time, his reply appears almost the second I've hit send.

**Sven_247** Yeah, if you want.

**Sven_247** Where do you want to meet?

**Sven_247** When?

The messages are just a touch too short, too quick.

My stomach is still stirring, but this time, he's going to do things on my terms. I'm going to decide where we meet. I'm going to confront him. But not before I've seen his phone and gotten the proof I need.

> **Chlo03** Saturday, by Ferrington Town park . . . 7 p.m.?

Sven sends a huge, happy smiley by way of response.
Got him.

# CHAPTER 39

## Amber

On the walk home from school, my bag keeps bashing against my lower back. I've not only got my workbooks in there, but my gym gear from this morning, so it's packed solid and keeps thumping with a dull rhythm as I walk along.

Ren still hasn't seen the message or replied. I'm resigned to the fact that he's never going to respond. Why would he? He has loads going on. Things way more interesting than anything in my life.

A little way in front of me, there's a familiar flash of royal-blue shirt and dark hair – which I recognize instantly as Ansh.

My feet freeze up.

*Oh God.* I *have* to walk this way. And I bet he thinks I'm a complete stalker. What do I do?

He hasn't messaged me since I let it slip that I knew stuff about him from his Instagram, and to be honest, I don't blame him. I should just keep walking behind him, but then again, what if he turns around and notices me? I know what to do: I'll just speed past him, my head down.

I can feel my pulse fluttering slightly as I step forward and walk as fast as I can in front of Ansh.

'Hey!' Ansh's deep voice calls after me.

I turn around, feeling my face drain of colour.

'Er, h-hey.' My voice cracks slightly as I speak.

He dips his head down and falls into step with me. But for some reason, he's barely looking at me – his dark eyes flickering off to the side.

'You all right?' he grunts.

'Yeah.'

There's an uncomfortably long pause where I don't know what to say. Then a thought pops into my head.

'I was just wondering.' I'm talking too quickly. 'You know what we were talking about before, with Jemma and Maisie? I know you told me not to go looking . . . but do you know anything else about what happened?'

Ansh doesn't look at me. Instead he purses his lips and looks up to the sky for several seconds.

I'm beginning to wonder if he heard me, but then he looks down with a frown.

'Why do you ask so many questions about Ren?'

I blink several times. 'Um, no reason.'

'Because he's your brother?'

I feel my cheeks flush. 'Um, yeah. I'm just – I just want to know what's going on.'

Ansh nods. 'What does your mum think?'

'My mum? Our mum? Me and Ren's . . .'

'Yeah.'

'Well, um, she's been OK. I don't know if she really knows the details.'

I'm finding it harder and harder to keep talking. Oh God, I shouldn't have asked that question. I look at the ground.

'It's OK. Sorry – we can talk about something else,' I mumble.

Ansh is just staring at me.

'It's fine,' he says. 'This is me now, anyway.'

He nods to smokers' lane. I bite my lip.

'Yeah, because I'm going a different way actually tonight. I'll head off . . .' My voice is so quiet, even I can barely hear it.

Besides, Ansh doesn't seem to be listening.

He shrugs. 'Yeah – see ya.'

Without waiting for me to say bye, he starts walking off. Then, almost as an afterthought, he spins round and shouts back, 'Oh, and good luck on your date.'

I stop in my tracks. 'Date?'

'Yeah, that's what you told Iulia, didn't you? That you're going on a date.' His eyes are squinting as he looks at me.

My heart starts to thud. 'You – you spoke to Iulia?'

Ansh half-smiles. 'Yeah, I did. Pretty funny, actually, because you said you were his sister. I thought she must have got it wrong. What kind of sister dates their brother?'

My mouth is incredibly dry. I gulp, but I don't know what to say . . . I don't know what to —

'I didn't . . . I'm not . . .' I trail off.

Ansh breathes out slowly. 'It's fine. Whatever.' He splays out his elbows in a kind of shrug, hands tucked into either pocket. 'Enjoy your date.'

He walks off, and I feel my stomach sink to the ground.

# CHAPTER 40

## *Chloe*

Over the next few days, it feels almost natural to slip back into messaging Sven almost every minute of every day. Every so often, his messages come through a bit too fast, a bit too frantic – but then I remember it's only for a couple of days. It's only until I can meet him, get his phone, and get this all sorted out.

Tom has noticed I keep texting someone else, so I said it was just me and Louise having a lot to talk about at the moment. I haven't told him anything about my plan. I feel like I mustn't tell anyone; I know he would try and talk me out of it. Or insist on coming along and ruin it all. But I'm sick of feeling afraid, worrying constantly about what's going to happen next. With Sven quite literally in my pocket, I feel the most relaxed I've felt in weeks.

Tom is lying back across his bed late one night when he gently brushes a curl off of my shoulder and smiles at me.

'See – I told you they'd give up.'

'Who?' I say, kissing his fingertips.

'You've even forgotten all about it! The person hacking your accounts.'

These words from Tom's lips make my stomach stir uneasily.

Tom raises his eyebrows. 'Didn't I say they'd give up?'

'Oh, yeah – I guess they have,' I mumble, looking away.

'I haven't been sent any more photos from spam accounts. And nothing's happened with school, Louise either, I'm guessing? It's great, isn't it?' says Tom.

There's something about the way he's looking at me that is making me uncomfortable.

'Mmm,' I say, not wanting to reply.

I squint off at the far wall.

There's a weird thought forming in my mind. Something so wrong that I immediately quash it, telling myself I'm being stupid. It couldn't possibly be another guy, could it? Someone even closer to me. Someone trying to get back together . . .

'Do you remember Sven? It was so weird before, how much he messaged you,' says Tom, looking directly at me.

I squirm. 'Can we – can we not talk about Sven?'

Tom shrugs. 'Yeah, sure. I just thought—'

'No.' My voice is firmer than I intended. 'I don't want to talk about it any more.'

Tom looks at me, his smooth brow crinkling. 'No worries. We don't have to chat about it if it upsets you. We can talk about anything, like—'

I stand up. 'I want to get home, actually. I've got some . . . Mum is asking where I am.'

Tom gets up too. 'Um, OK.'

There's a beat of silence.

'Do you want me to walk you?' he says.

'No – no! It's fine.'

Tom leans forward, and I let him give me a kiss on the cheek. I pull away quickly and walk, alone, out of the room.

When I glance back, he's still standing in the same spot, staring at me.

# CHAPTER 41

## *Amber*

On Saturday morning, I'm cocooned in a duvet upstairs in my bedroom while a group of Seb's friends crash about downstairs. Their deep voices echo through the thin walls, but my mind is so loud, it's almost like I can't hear them.

I feel so, so stupid for lying to Ansh. Obviously he was going to find out I wasn't Ren's sister. Why did I even say that?

And it's pointless, anyway. It's not like any of my lies have even helped Ren. For the last twenty-four hours, my thoughts have been going round in circles, trying to work out whether Jemma and Iulia have got it right about Ren, and if not – why wouldn't they just say it was Jerome?

Could he have convinced them that Ren deserves it? Were they all drunk and just don't remember which guy? Could . . . could Jerome have nudes from when they dated and be *blackmailing* them?

I close my eyes and rub the side of my nose. There's a sheen

185

of grease that sticks to my thumb, and I can feel little raised bumps of tiny spots across my forehead.

It's 11 a.m. I haven't showered yet, so I feel a bit gross, but it doesn't really seem important. I catch sight of my reflection in my phone screen and turn it over so I don't have to look at myself.

I just wish, *wish* I could speak to Ren. I wish I could know what's going on and if he's OK. Not knowing whether he's innocent or guilty feels like it's slowly driving me insane.

I've read every Tweet that Ren has posted since he got Twitter two years ago. Every Instagram post since he started posting photos a year ago. I've clicked through his Facebook and looked up his family. I've gone through the profile of every friend who's ever visited the gym with him, every girl called Jemma, Maisie or Iulia on his friends list.

But . . . there's nothing.

I sit there, chewing at a loose hangnail. It tears, and a blob of blood trickles down my thumb.

Right – that's it. I've been doing this all morning. I need a break.

I push myself away from my laptop and tiptoe downstairs, craning my neck to hear whether Seb's friends are in the kitchen. I'm pretty sure they've all gone outside; their voices are muffled and distant.

I know I look disgusting, shuffling around in my grey nightshirt and flannel trousers, but it's not like I've had time to get dressed this morning. I literally spent all night at the computer, and as soon as I got out of bed, I immediately began to check Ren's pages to see if I'd missed anything.

It almost feels like I've had an exam.

In the living room, Mum is standing there with a hand on one hip, dressed in a white dress, her bushy dark hair tumbling prettily over her shoulders.

She's frowning at the TV and jabbing buttons on the remote.

'Bloody smart TV!' she snaps. 'All I want to do is see Sylvia's daughter's wedding video! I have it on the computer – why can't I watch it?' When she sees me, her eyes widen. 'Amber! Do you know how to get the computer to cast to the TV?'

'Erm . . .' I back away slowly towards the kitchen. I do know how to do that on my laptop, but with Mum's old PC, it will probably take me all morning to get it set up.

'Ugh!' Mum sighs, dropping the remote onto the sofa.

Slowly, I step into the kitchen and start boiling the kettle. I'm about to ask Mum if she wants a tea, when there's an almighty shriek from the next room.

I roll my eyes to the ceiling. What has she done now?

She shouts again, and I hear Seb clattering in through the front door. I freeze, straining my ears. But I only heard one set of footsteps – the rest of his friends must still be outside. Gingerly I step back into the living room.

'Mum, are you OK . . .' My eye catches sight of the TV, and the words die on my tongue.

Mum looks like she's seen a ghost. She's stabbing at the remote, horrified.

'What is going on?' she shouts. 'Who is this man?'

Plastered across the giant screen, in full technicolour, is my laptop screen. There are six overlapping tabs open – one for each of Ren's social media sites; several others open on his posts from a year ago; and yet another open on a conversation between him and Iulia from two months ago.

187

Seb grabs the remote off her.

'Here, Mum – you can take it off like this.'

'B-but I don't understand! Why are there so many pictures of that man? Whose computer is it?'

Seb briefly looks up and catches my eye. I can feel that all the colour has drained from my face.

He rubs his temples. 'Look. I don't think . . .' Seb looks up, then sighs, indicating towards me. 'Ask her,' is all he says, switching off the TV screen so it flickers back to the sign-in screen.

Mum frowns, turning to me. 'Ask you? I don't get it. Amber, do you know why there are so many pictures of that man on the screen?'

Seb has dropped the remote on the floor and is making his way back out into the garden.

Mum's eyes flick from the screen to me, and back again. A vein pulses in her forehead.

'Oh God, have you . . . Have you met someone? Online?'

'No, no – it's not that. It's—'

Seb has reappeared at the door. Behind him, I can see several of his friends, and I have the uncontrollable urge to dissolve.

'Yeah, Amber – why don't you tell her,' he says drily, and my stomach twists. 'Tell her why you're stalking Ren Moore.'

# CHAPTER 42

## Amber

Mum's eyes widen, and a lock of wavy hair falls in front of her ear.

'Ren Moore? That boy who does the machines at the gym?' She stares at me, her mouth open. 'You're *stalking* him?'

'No!' I can hear Seb's friends chattering outside, and a couple of them glance through the patio doors at me.

Mum follows my gaze and grabs my arm. 'Amber, what – what is going on?'

'Everything's fine!' I snap, wrenching my arm away.

'Then why are you *stalking someone*?' She almost whispers the last words, her eyes wide with concern.

'I'm not – I'm not *doing that*,' I say. Then I pause. What do I say? That I'm trying to prove he's innocent? That he's assaulted loads of girls? Yeah, that's going to make Mum less worried.

'It's just . . . It's not like that. Seb just put those pictures up because he thinks I fancy him. As a joke. I'm . . . friends with Ren. We go to the gym together.'

Mum opens her mouth to speak again, but I cut her off.

'Anyway, I've got to go and do some homework,' I say, almost running upstairs. When I look back, I see Mum staring after me, biting her lip.

As I close my bedroom door, I hear her talking loudly on the phone, probably calling Dad. I rush over to my desk and disconnect all my casting settings. Then I slump in the chair and put my head in my hands.

A tear dribbles down my nose as I think about how pathetic I am. How pointless these last few weeks have been. How I am never, ever going to know what happened.

And maybe . . . I just need to come to terms with that.

My phone is unlocked beside me, open on Ren's Snap Map icon.

There's a soft creak from my bedroom door, which almost makes me jump up and scrape my knee across my desk.

Seb is standing there, his head tilted to one side.

I turn away from him, not wanting him to see my tears. 'Leave me alone,' I say.

There's a sigh, and I hear him step forward into the room, closing the door behind him with a click.

'You've got to stop this,' he says quietly.

'Leave me alone,' I say again, but this time my voice is a whisper, and I can't even finish the sentence without my shoulders heaving.

'Honestly, sis, you've—'

'You don't understand,' I say, watching a tear fall onto my desk. 'He's not – It's not what you . . . Ren is innocent. It was Jerome – I'm sure of it.'

Seb frowns. 'What was Jerome?'

'The guy who assaulted Chloe at the party. I think he assaulted the other girls too, I think—'

'It wasn't Jerome,' says Seb flatly, cutting me off.

I look at him for the first time. 'It could have been! It—'

'No. Jerome was buddied up with Nick in beer pong that night. He threw up about five times, barely made it to 10 p.m. before Bill had to take him home.'

I blink at him.

There's a crash of noise downstairs, and several of Seb's friends start shouting his name.

Seb glances at the door. 'Look. Whatever you're doing, cut it out. Ren is bad news. And this . . .' He looks down at my unwashed hair and pale, drawn face. 'It's not good for you.'

Seb turns around and heads back towards the noise and chatter of his friends. It's only once he's gone that I notice my pulse drumming against my temple.

My mind is whirling.

I know he's right. I need to stop. I blink a couple of times as my vision blurs.

I need to stop.

. . . *But I can't.*

On autopilot, I glance at my phone screen. Ren's Snapchat map icon is lit up. The dot of his location spinning around in a nearby village, moving quickly. He must be on a bus or something.

I rub my temples, hard, with my thumb.

Ren's blob dances around on my screen.

The problem is, before I can stop, I need to *know*. So, if Jerome didn't assault those girls . . . someone else did.

And I know that the dates don't match up for either Jemma

191

or Iulia's stories, but I don't know anything else. There's not even a trail online between Ren and Maisie. I mean, did they even really meet?

*How do I know what's real any more?*

I stare, hard, at the moving blob on my screen. An uneasy thought is beginning to form in my mind. If he keeps his location on, if he stays online, I'll know where he is.

My heart starts to thump.

The longer he doesn't clear his name, the more people are going to believe he actually did it. And I know he didn't. Well, for two of them, there's doubt, at least. And if I actually speak to him, I'm sure I can prove it was, in fact, Jerome who did it.

I picture Ren's kind, smiling face, and it almost breaks my heart to think of him jobless and alone.

*I just can't let this happen.*

At that moment, the blob starts doing something strange. A second ago, it was one village away; now it seems to be making a beeline for our town. My eyes widen.

Staring at the avatar, I watch, dumbfounded, as in jerky movements it speeds up, heading closer and closer towards me.

For one giddy moment, I imagine he's coming to my house. He knows that I can help him. Maybe . . . maybe he just wants to see me. I imagine Mum's face when he shows up. I imagine Seb's. And Seb's friends'.

I watch the screen for a solid thirty minutes, and now the blob has come so close, he's mere streets away. I almost feel like I'm daydreaming. Like this is some bizarre fantasy where Ren is going to walk in, come upstairs, and ask me to help him. Then I'll show him what I've found, we'll take it to the gym manager together, and end up kissing as we celebrate him getting his job back.

My lip starts to tremble.

The blob has stopped now, near the skatepark. He's so close, I could just walk over and see him. Tell him about Iulia and Jemma's mismatched dates. Ask him about Maisie.

I can still hear Mum talking in concerned, hushed tones to Dad downstairs. I ignore her and slip into the bathroom.

Five minutes later, red-faced after having had the quickest shower known to man, I throw my laptop into a backpack, pick up my phone, and stare at the location.

Ren's icon winks at me.

Yep. He's still there. Still at the park.

Honestly, what choice do I have?

# CHAPTER 43

## *Chloe*

What are you supposed to wear to confront your stalker? It feels almost like a date. Some weird, sick date that is also somehow your worst nightmare.

If Sven does show up, then I want him to think that for me, this is a genuine date. At least for long enough to pinch his phone and slip it into my pocket.

He's only ever seen Instagram photos of me – which is me looking at my absolute best. He also said I was a 'slut' in that tight, sequinned green dress.

A shiver runs down my spine at the memory.

I need to look good, but not too good. Usually tight, low-cut tops and short skirts make me feel confident – but recently all I've been wearing are loose jeans and hoodies. I pull on an old mauve vintage dress, which plunges down to reveal my cleavage, and feel slightly sick.

There's a sudden flashback to the feeling of J grabbing my

breast out of my dress, mingled with the sound of Sven chanting '*slut, slut, slut*'.

I throw off the dress and turn away from the mirror, not wanting to look at my bare body in the reflection.

In the end, I compromise by plumping for a tight, grey roll-neck dress.

It shows off every twist and curve – it looks like Instagram me; like I've made an effort. But everything is covered. It's long-sleeved, and I'm wearing thick woolly tights, so there's not an inch of me on show.

Shrugging on my favourite denim jacket, I swing my small backpack over my shoulders and grit my teeth.

This is it. This is the day I catch him.

The day all of this *stops*.

*** 

On the walk towards the spot in the park where we've agreed to meet at, my feet start to slow down.

What if I can't actually do this? What if he's like J, but worse, and just overpowers me completely?

What if he knows my whole 'accounts being deactivated' excuse is a load of crap?

*What if it's not even Sven who shows up?*

Gnawing the inside of my cheek, I run through the plan one more time in my mind to try and steady my nerves.

Go up to him. Act like it's a date. Be friendly. Flirty. Giggle. Gauge how dangerous this guy really is.

My teeth start to chatter.

Talk to him. Don't mention Tom. Or any ex-boyfriend. If he asks, just be vague. Or say Tom is your cousin. Or gay.

I pull the dress sleeves over my fingertips.

Once he's distracted, take out your phone. Show him some selfies. Maybe put your arm around him, if you can bear it. When he puts his phone down, subtly pick it up.

I've unbuttoned my tiny backpack in preparation so it'll be easy to slip his phone inside.

But what if he keeps his phone on him the whole time?

There's one thing I can do that will almost definitely work: I could kiss him. That would definitely distract him long enough for me to take his phone.

My stomach starts to clench uncomfortably, both with repulsion and nerves.

*What about Tom?*

Oh, screw it. What am I even thinking? I won't have to kiss him. It'll be absolutely fine. I know how to distract men. It'll be easy. I will be able to get his phone.

The wind whips around my ankles. There's a couple of stray crisp packets wrapping round the metal swing gate to the park. I cross my arms over my chest and walk through them. The bars give an eerie creak, which makes the hairs on my arms stand on end.

My hearts thumps harder in my chest as I approach the skatepark.

This is where we agreed to meet. I'm a couple of minutes late, so he'll probably already be there. I keep my head down as I approach. Taking a low breath, I skim the surrounding area with my gaze.

I stop walking.

There's no one here.

A tension is gently unknotting in my stomach. It almost feels like relief. Almost, but not quite.

*Is he late?*

Glancing behind me, I go and sit on the bench closest to the skatepark.

My eyes survey the bushes flanking either side of the tarmacked skate rink.

A wind rustles the leaves in the bush to my left. My face freezes.

Did I just see –

Is there someone *hiding* behind that bush?

I swallow and blink again. Fast.

But I can't see anything. Or anyone. The park is silent.

I look down at my phone. No messages.

My fingers are shaking as they swipe the screen.

Oh, screw this.

Seriously, screw this.

If he is hiding somewhere watching me, then we're never going to meet. There's no point feeling scared. If he comes, he comes.

*And if he doesn't . . .*

Well, then he doesn't.

Clamping my hands tightly to my phone, I stand up, readjust my dress, and march over to the bushes directly behind the skatepark.

Awkwardly, I kneel down so my body is completely obscured by the foliage and separate a branch of leaves so I can peer directly onto the nearest bench.

Then I sit.

Waiting.

# CHAPTER 44

# *Amber*

My teeth are chattering so hard, it feels like my whole head is vibrating. I try to purse my lips to stop them from shaking, but I almost bite the end of my tongue.

The air is cool against my cheeks, and icy against my wet hair.

Oh *God*, I should have worn something different. I should have put on some make-up, or at least dried my hair so it wasn't still soaking. Individual strands are starting to dry now in weird, curling wisps across my face. I tuck them behind my ear, wishing I had a hairband.

Surreptitiously, I pull out my phone and glance at Ren's location. I've taken several screenshots in case my internet signal cuts out or he goes offline, but so far, his blob is in the same place.

I actually know where he is in *real* time.

My whole body is trembling from head to toe. It's been almost a month since I last saw him, that time at the gym when he rested his hand gently on my shoulder. It almost doesn't feel real that I'm about to see his kind face again. I can't stop my stomach from twisting, my hands from fidgeting, my lips from trembling.

I look up.

A horrible thought twists into my mind.

Do you think he'll actually be there? Could I have somehow got his location wrong?

*Is this all a complete waste of time?*

I'm getting closer now. His dot is almost on top of mine.

Glancing up, I catch sight of a dark-haired guy in front of me, walking along. It takes a second for the sight to sink in, but then my entire body reacts, feeling like it's on fire.

With a silent yelp, I scramble behind the nearest bush along the skatepark.

My stomach twisting, I peer out of the foliage, my knees scraping across the dry ground.

He's just walking along, dressed all in black. He looks different to how he usually looks in gym gear. Not how I'd imagined his non-work clothes – cooler, somehow.

He turns to face the wind, and I see his profile.

My stomach somersaults way up into my chest.

It's definitely him.

Definitely. *Definitely*.

He goes and sits on one of the benches. In the distance, there's a stunning girl walking towards the same park benches, squinting at her phone. She's dressed in a skintight roll-neck dress, which clings to every curve of her body.

I look down at my baggy ensemble. I can't believe some people actually look like that. That their body curves in such a perfect, toned way, that their hair – so dark and glossy – falls over their shoulders like . . .

Wait a second.

I stand up from my spot and try to crane my neck closer.

Is that . . .?

OH-MY-GOD!

It is. *Chloe*. It's Chloe MacNeil.

The closer I get, the easier it is to her characteristically high cheekbones. Her full, red lips. Her dark cat-like eyes.

No one else has such a distinctive look.

Oh *God*, what if she sees me speaking to Ren?

But before I have time to think about that, my mouth drops open.

Chloe is walking. Quicker now, closer and closer.

But she's not coming to me.

She's moving in the opposite direction, walking towards Ren, her hips swinging prettily from side to side like she's on a catwalk.

And it feels like my whole world is crashing around my ears.

# CHAPTER 45

# *Chloe*

It's been fifteen minutes, and there's still no one here. I keep thinking the bush on the other side of the park is moving – but I can't tell if there's really someone there or I'm just going insane.

My knees are beginning to ache. I daren't sit down completely in case I get grass stains on my dress, but I have to keep low to the ground, otherwise my head will peep up higher than the bushes.

I nibble the corner of my lip. The wind is making them dry and scratchy. I'm about to reach into my bag and pull out some lip balm when I stop.

Why does it *matter* if my lips are dry?

I drop the tube back into my bag and shift my legs so I'm putting my weight on the less-stiff knee. How long should I wait before I leave? Another five minutes?

My fingers brush a clump of dried mud off my tights. I'm not even paying attention when, through the foliage, I glimpse a tall guy in black tracksuit trousers, a jumper and a beanie hat pulled low over his face. He goes and sits on the bench, his head down.

*Oh my God! Could it be . . .?*

From this angle, I can't make out his face. His jumper has a high neck, and his hat is so low, there's only a glimpse of tanned skin showing.

He pulls out his mobile.

Almost instantly my phone buzzes with a message.

> **Sven_247** Here.

> **Sven_247** Where are you?

Crap. He's going to hear the vibrations.

I stab at the screen, but he starts sending more messages, and it buzzes incessantly.

There's nothing for it. I'm going to have to go over before he hears.

I leap up and brush away the blades of grass, stuck hair-like to my tights. Then I purse my lips together and step out so I'm facing him.

He's still staring at his screen. I feel weirdly self-conscious. He's only ever seen my Instagram photos, and I look way worse in real life.

What if he's disgusted by the real me?

Well, then I guess that's good. Maybe he'll stop harassing me. Or maybe he'll hate me even more. Like those angry guys online who say girls who wear make-up are 'liars' who are 'tricking them' into thinking they're hot. I mean, as if anyone has black-ringed eyes and green sparkly eyeshadow naturally, anyway.

My heart is beating faster and faster.

He hasn't looked up from his phone yet, his fingers still jabbing at the screen. My phone is twitching nonstop in my pocket. It takes all the will in the world for me not to just bolt. But I keep walking towards him, until I'm about a metre away.

He glances up momentarily – his lips are full, his nose flat, and his dark eyebrows handsomely arched. His mouth falls open when he sees me, and his face kind of jerks in surprise.

His admiring expression makes my chest puff out.

'Hey,' I say, hiding my chattering teeth with a broad smile. 'It's me!' I force myself to give a little giggle.

'Hey.' His voice is low, gruff – and he speaks downwards, into his chest. He hunches himself inwards under the baggy material, and I realize that he's seriously built underneath his jumper.

*Why are his clothes so loose?*

'Chloe?' His voice is so low, I can barely make out the words he's saying.

I smile, and I can start to feel my old self filtering through the nerves. I can do this.

'Sven! I can't believe it's you.' I smile and sit right next to him. Close. My eyes swivel to his phone, which he immediately drops into his tracksuit pocket. Damn.

'Um, yeah, I—' He kind of chokes on his words as he speaks.

I eye him calmly, and two spots of pink appear on each of his tanned cheeks.

He clears his throat. 'Wanna – I dunno – go for a walk?'

I nod. He stands up, much taller than I was expecting, and there's something about the way he moves that puts me on edge.

He keeps fidgeting with the collar of his jumper. And twitching like there's a bug on his cheek.

I smooth my dress down over my hips as I stand up. When I raise my eyes, he's staring at my hands.

'Shall we head this way?' I say politely.

He's so quiet, and jumpy, that I feel the knot in my stomach start to loosen. I don't know what I was expecting, exactly. But not someone who couldn't meet my eye. He's very tall – way over six foot – but walks as though apologetic for his height, his head bent, chest slumped.

'You look nice,' he says as a grunt.

It takes me a couple of seconds to decipher his mumbled words.

'Oh, thanks.'

I catch his eye, and he immediately looks away.

The hairs on the back of my arm tighten.

I don't know whether to laugh or cry.

# CHAPTER 46

## Amber

I should just turn around.

Right now, I should just get up, walk off, and let them have their date.

But I can't stop myself from following them.

The wind is battering against my ears. My fingertips are turning blue from the cold, and my wet hair has become a block of ice against my neck. But it's like some weird, sick fascination. My feet follow their steps almost independently. As though I'm a puppet and there's someone else pulling the strings.

Of course he would be meeting Chloe.

Who wouldn't? She's probably the prettiest and most confident girl you could ever met. Just like everyone who meets Ren falls in love with him – everyone who meets Chloe falls in love with her.

In a way, they're the perfect match.

But, my God, I've been *so stupid*.

How could I ever think he'd want my help? How could I

think that spending all those hours trying to prove his innocence would make him want to talk to me?

I'm starting to feel my stomach stir.

Did I only do it because I liked him? Was I hoping I would help him get his job back and he'd be so delighted, he would fall in love with me?

*. . . Was Seb right?*

Chloe and Ren have their heads together and are saying something quietly to one another. She's leading him down the path, towards a clearing in the park.

There's a creeping feeling across my skin. I shouldn't keep following them; I should just go home.

As they disappear beyond the clearing, I stop.

*What am I actually doing?* Following two people who are on a date and don't even know I exist.

My eyes start to fill with tears.

And then it hits me. Until I saw Ren with Chloe, I never realized how many of my daily thoughts were about him. How often I dreamed of when he touched my shoulder. How many times I fantasized about the moment I would see him again and tell him that I believed him.

Now I think back to that smile at the gym. The memory I've replayed so many times, it doesn't even feel real. I no longer know what is actual memory and what is fantasy – but now, in my mind, the smile is a brief flicker of acknowledgment. A polite nod from someone just doing their job.

Nothing, really.

Certainly not something anyone should think about every minute of every day. Refreshing his online profiles. Again and again and again.

I stare out across the edge of the clearing. There's an icy silence, which lets my horrible thoughts ring out loud.

*Stupid. Stupid. Stupid—*

There's a muffled scream.

I blink. What?

It was faint, barely a whisper. But I heard it. It was definitely a scream.

*Am I going mad?*

But then I hear a man's voice, strangled against the wind.

Ren?!

Without thinking about what my feet are doing, I run towards them.

# CHAPTER 47

## Chloe

I've managed to tease some conversation out of Sven. Just general things, like where he works out, what he's doing at college. As we talk, he seems to become more fidgety. He keeps moving his arms beneath his baggy jumper, and he's so . . . tense. Every few steps, he'll flick an imaginary bit of fluff off his jumper or jolt his shoulder unexpectedly.

As we're walking along, I have a flashback to us texting late at night right at the start. How intimate it felt. How much I felt like I knew him. His bronzed face is fixated on the ground now. An uneasy feeling creeps into my stomach.

How much did I *really* know him?

Why did I stay up all night messaging a complete stranger like that?

But the more we talk, the more unsure I am that Sven is the one behind everything that's been happening. He just seems so shy. He doesn't seem like the type to hack into my school emails, send false messages to Louise. And besides, he wouldn't have even *had* those photos.

I glance up. His *slut* comments flashing before my eyes.

Is he *really* the one behind all of this?

I just . . . can't picture it.

I laugh at something Sven says to try to relax him. His whole face lights up. I half-smile back.

This whole situation feels like a very young, very awkward first date.

'It's strange meeting someone you've only spoken to in person for the first time, don't you think,' I say, smiling. With each step, my nerves are beginning to melt away. This guy isn't dangerous. He's more nervous than me by a mile.

The problem is, I still can't get anywhere near his phone. He's been holding on to it ever since we met and glances at it every few seconds. There's no way he's going to put it down without realizing. How can I find out for sure whether he's the one behind the messages? I need evidence.

We find a place to sit on a grassy slope, and Sven leans his arms forward, resting them against his parted knees. I curl my legs up underneath me and turn towards him.

'It's really nice to have finally met you,' I say, and I look directly into his eye.

He blushes and his eyes dart either side of me. 'Yeah. I mean – yeah, it's nice.' He clears his throat. 'You look, y'know, really good.' His eyes sweep over the curve of my chest.

I try to smile back, but a thought is forming in my mind. A memory so vivid, it stings: me pouring my heart out to him about what happened with J. The fear I felt when he didn't reply. The message: *WHORE*.

212

I glance down at my phone. I definitely saw him type the texts to me earlier. I know this is his correct number. He's the one who sent those messages.

I might not know if he hacked my life, but I know one thing: he's the guy who called me a whore.

He's talking to me now – in stuttered tones – about some workout he does at the gym. I nod, trying to pay attention, but inside me, there's a burning sensation kindling, rising up through my veins.

*Slut. Whore.*

The unfairness of the last few weeks comes crashing over me like a tidal wave. The shame put on me by him, the guy from the party, and even my friends.

Interrupting our conversation, I give a loud snort.

Sven stops taking mid-sentence. 'Are you OK?' he says, holding my gaze.

'Yeah, yeah – I'm fine.'

'OK,' he says, and he starts talking again.

I hold up my hand. 'Actually, you know what? I don't think I am OK.'

I look him square in the eye, and he blinks several times.

'Why did – before, when we were texting, and I told you about that guy – why did you call me a slut?'

Sven's eyes widen, but then he looks away.

'I already apologized for that,' he says, his tone a touch defensive. His bottom lip curls at the corner.

'Yeah, I know. But I don't get why you said it in the first place. When a girl tells you someone assaulted her, why is your first response to make it her fault?'

Sven looks up to the sky, then glances back at my legs. 'I said sorry.'

There's an edge to his quiet voice now. And no stutter. But I press on.

'And this weird thing happened. When my, um, phone deleted you, my friend Louise showed me these strange messages I'd never sent. Between me and this guy she was seeing.'

Sven looks at me sharply.

'The thing is I've never even spoken to this guy. The messages were completely made up.'

Out of the corner of my eye, I can see his teeth grit.

'Don't you think that's weird?' I say, my voice rising higher.

He clears his throat. 'Yeah, I guess.'

I can't stop myself from talking. 'And at school everyone got sent Louise's private photos. From *my* email address, though I don't remember sending them.' I stare right at him. 'It's been really, actually, weird.'

Sven isn't looking at me any more. He's looking straight down in between his clasped-together arms, his eyes running along the floor. His face twitches – and I can just about make out the muscles of his jaw clenching and unclenching.

'Do you have anything to say about that?'

He looks up, his face set. Suddenly his tense cheeks slacken – and he speaks so quietly, it's almost a whisper.

'Why did you bring me here, Chloe?'

# CHAPTER 48

## Chloe

Sven's words whistle across the empty clearing, the sun gently filtering through the leaves of the trees either side of us.

'Why did I *bring you here*?' I repeat, confused.

I don't know how to answer. Whether I should pretend to keep flirting with him, or if the charade is really up.

Sven's eyes flash. 'Why did you bring me here when you have a *boyfriend*.' He almost spits the last word out, and for the first time, I see venom in his trembling face.

'A *boyfriend*?'

I keep thinking about all the things I planned to say – that Tom was my cousin, or a friend – but all the pretence is draining out of me.

This guy has made my life a misery. I deserve to know why.

I suck in my breath. 'So what if I have a boyfriend? I can speak to other guys. I can meet up with other guys. His name is Tom Taylor, by the way – but I'm guessing you already knew that!'

My lip curls as I look at him. I can't believe this is the guy I confided in. The person I messaged almost every minute of every day for a while. The person I kept secret from Tom.

How could I have been so *stupid*?

'Aaaargh!' Sven suddenly, violently, clutches the sides of his head. 'I knew it, you bitch! I knew you had a boyfriend.'

His eyes are directly on me now. Intense. Red.

My heart starts to beat wildly.

'I never said I didn't have a boyfriend!' I feel my body shrinking away from him.

'But you messaged me! You got with that guy at the party. You might as well have got with Jerome!'

It's like my veins have been plunged into ice.

'I didn't say the messages at school were about someone called Jerome.'

There's a beat of silence. My mind starts working in over-drive. There were tagged Instagram photos of me and Louise together that night. There were comments between Jerome and Louise underneath the pictures. On Tom's friends' accounts there were pictures of them both, videos and stories of us all from the party.

Did he *guess* from all that?

Sven looks straight at me, and I suddenly feel very, *very* scared.

'I should never have apologized,' he spits. 'You know exactly what type of girl you are. *Exactly*.'

I can feel my whole body fold up into itself. He seems wild with fury.

'You would never bother with a guy like me! I'm a nice guy – I messaged you every day! I never kept you waiting or treated you like crap—'

He leans forwards and grabs me by the shoulders with both hands. I let out a tiny scream, but then look around. There's no one here – we're flanked by trees either side. No one can hear or see me.

Oh God. Why didn't I tell anyone what I was doing? What's going to happen?

Can I talk him round, somehow? Oh God. Fuck.

*What have I done?!*

Sven is still speaking, screaming in my face. 'You message me constantly! You lead me on with those photographs on Instagram! Well you don't get to do that. You don't get to behave like a complete slut and get away with it.'

He's shouting loudly now, his voice shaking. He grips my shoulders, pinning my arms either side of my body. I can feel the pressure of his hot grip, pushing me down on the grass.

I squirm, but this only seems to make him angrier.

'It's not fair! It's just not fair!' he shouts.

I'm shaking all over. I can feel tears springing from my eyes, but I can't control them.

*OhGodOhGodOhGod.*

'I'm sorry,' I choke, trying to make him stop. 'I shouldn't have invited you here.'

'YOU SHOULDN'T HAVE BLOCKED ME IN THE FIRST PLACE!' His voice echoes down the park. 'I gave you everything! Any time of day, I was there for you! What more could you possibly want?'

His nails are digging into my bones. I can feel the force behind his arms – the strength hidden by his baggy jumper. My heart is drumming frantically in my chest – my breath coming in short, desperate bursts.

'GET OFF HER!' Suddenly there's a high-pitched cry from someone nearby.

Oh, thank God. Thank God. Thank God!

Sven looks up, and all of a sudden, a log comes crashing down behind him.

# CHAPTER 49

# *Amber*

They can't see me, but I can see them. Over the top of the clearing, there are two figures, kneeling down in an embrace.

But wait – it's not an embrace.

I step forward and see Chloe's eyes, big and wide. Ren is clutching her shoulders, his hands pinning her arms to her side.

She looks tiny. Not tiny like thin, beautiful. Tiny like frail. Like a breakable doll.

'*I'm sorry!*' I see her mouth against the rattle of the wind.

It feels like everything is happening in slow motion.

I see the real Ren for the first time. Him following Maisie home after they've been on a few dates. Her terrified face when he won't leave. I see him being forceful with Jemma after their night out, pushing her to go further. Him pinning Iulia to the ground. I can feel his fingers on them, his skin-crawling touch like nails against a chalkboard.

His face is changing. His beautiful eyes are flashing with

anger, and it's almost like his pretty features are being rearranged before my eyes. I feel a jolt of repulsion.

He was guilty.

*I was wrong.*

Ren starts screaming in Chloe's face. His mouth twisted in a horrible grimace. His arms, with deep muscles bulging out of them, don't look strong; they look weak.

He looks ugly.

Chloe, too, looks different. Usually she's the most animated person in the room, but here, her eyes are wide. Her body is tiny and crumpled like a child's.

My heart starts to beat. Really, really fast.

I feel a twist of disdain in the pit of my stomach. I feel a fury building like when Seb and I used to have screaming matches as little children. A wild, uncontrollable anger.

*He can't do this.*

And I won't let him. Not again. Not to another girl.

Without thinking what my feet are doing, I run forward. Neither of them sees me. Chloe has lowered her gaze to the ground, and Ren is looking straight at her.

'YOU SHOULDN'T HAVE BLOCKED ME IN THE FIRST PLACE!'

Ren is screaming now. He looks crazed, his eyes red, sweat dripping down his face.

The blood is thumping through my veins. A flashback to childhood. Playfighting with Seb. He was always bigger than me, but that didn't mean he always won.

When he pinned me down, what did I do? How did I stop him?

My mind is whirring as I look round the park for something,

anything. I grab a log. Heavier than I was expecting. Then, with a heave, I lift it up above me. Not above his head or neck, that would be mad. But high above his shoulders.

Something makes me stop. Maybe I won't have to. Maybe he'll just stop.

Maybe he won't . . .

But I need to be sure. In my left hand, I unlock my phone, swipe open the video camera and click record.

'GET OFF HER!' I shout, and Chloe's eyes lift up to mine in shock.

Ren doesn't drop her. I see his grip tighten on her arms, his nails biting deep into her skin. He looks up, and his eyes don't even seem to flicker with acknowledgement.

'Get the fuck away from us!' he shouts, rocking Chloe's whole body with his fists.

My stomach twists as I throw the log as hard as I can, down onto the ground.

# CHAPTER 50

## Amber

I'm standing over Ren, my chest rising and falling, sweat dripping off my nose. I look down at him. He hasn't moved.

'Get off her!' I shout again, and I'm surprised by how strongly my voice carries across the field.

Ren keeps hold of Chloe. Why won't he let her go?

I heave up the log over my shoulder again, ready to slam it down to the ground beside them.

'What the hell are you doing, you psycho?!' shrieks Ren, leaping up.

He steps forward aggressively, and his eyes snap on me. He's so close, I can see every freckle, line and vein on his face. My heart starts to beat, fast.

I have spent hours looking at his face every day, several times a day.

But he doesn't look how he looked online. He looks better, but also worse. Behind his eyes, I can see the flash of fury. I'm seeing Ren, but not my Ren. Not the one I created in my head.

The Ren that never existed.

'It's you!' His mouth twists with disgust. 'Weird girl from the gym.'

My heart stops.

*Weird girl from the gym?*

Even though I know my Ren wasn't real, even though I know everything I thought about him was wrong, the phrase still makes my eyes widen.

'Weird?' I say quietly.

'You just almost hit me with a fucking log!' he spits, and Chloe shrinks away from him.

But I don't shrink away. He's twice my size and has muscles bulging out of his shirt, but I don't feel scared; I feel *furious*. Absolutely fucking furious.

I can't believe that someone can behave like this. That someone can be so entitled that he thinks he can just take what he wants. That someone can act nice to me when he's actually awful. That he calls me 'weird' and 'psycho' just because I stopped him behaving like a monster.

'And you think that's worse?'

Ren steps forward. 'What the—'

'You think me throwing a log is worse than what you did to those girls? What you did to Chloe?'

Ren scoffs. 'I didn't do anything to her. She's the one leading guys on, posting selfies, flirting with everyone. She's a fucking—'

'Why can't she do that?' I say.

I rise to my full height and puff out my chest.

'What's wrong with flirting? What's wrong with wanting attention? It's harmless. She's not hurting anyone . . .'

'It's disgusting!' he shouts.

224

Chloe has stood up now and is next to me, standing very close. I can feel the warmth of her body beside me, and it emboldens me.

'Why? *You* do it.'

'What?!' he says, turning on me.

'You flirt with girls, at the gym. You lead them on,' I say, louder than I was expecting.

Ren laughs. 'Oh, for God's sake. That's not the same.'

'Just leave,' says Chloe, all of a sudden.

Her voice is so quiet, it's almost a whisper. I've never heard her speak like that.

Ren swivels to face her, and I feel her arm tense up next to mine.

'You're pathetic. You're a slut. You don't deserve someone who's going to treat you well. You deserve—'

'JUST GO!' I shout, the volume of my voice surprising even me. I step in front of Chloe so he can't get to her. 'Leave us! NOW!'

Ren's eyes glance at the log in my right arm and my phone in my left. 'You're pathetic,' he says.

But it's an empty insult. I can see in his eye, he's beat.

'So what if I am?' I step forward.

Ren glares at me and then snorts. 'No guy would like you, anyway. You're absolutely disgusting. Both of you.'

'Yeah, right. Tell that to the police.'

My voice is high and artificially cheery. I step forward, and Ren takes a step back, glaring at me.

'Run away, then. Bye!' I'm shouting after him as he walks away. I don't stop shouting, I keep walking forward, my arm with

225

my phone outstretched, recording. He spits on the floor and rolls his eyes.

Blood is pumping through my veins. As I watch him slope off, I can almost physically feel the weight of all those hours melt away. Hours spent looking at his social media, creating the perfect man in my mind, imagining someone that never was.

It feels like everything has evaporated apart from the earth I'm standing on. But what's left, the bit that I can actually feel, is solid.

When I turn to look at Chloe, she's standing there with her mouth open, staring up at me.

# CHAPTER 51

## *Chloe*

There's a low rustle as the wind sweeps across the open grass, separating the bracken. We both stand there, our chests rising and falling.

I'm shaking all over. Every time I try to steady my breath, my chest tightens, and my mouth makes a loud, rasping sob.

'Are – are you OK?' says a quiet voice.

Amber Nighy is standing there in front of me, plucking at the hem of her woolly dark purple cardigan. She has a large pus-filled whitehead on the tip of her nose, and her forehead gleams in the low sunlight, but her chin is tilted up, her shoulders square.

My eyes begin to fill with tears.

'I don't – I don't know.' I shake my head. 'He's been stalking me. Online. I'm just *so* scared. Now this has happened, what's he going to do next?'

I'm almost just talking to myself, gnawing the inside of my cheek.

Amber comes next to me, standing so close, we're almost touching.

'He's not going to do anything,' she says.

I sniff. 'W-why not?'

'Look at this.' Amber pulls out her phone screen, clicks on a video, and presses play.

Immediately the screen springs into life. You can clearly see Sven standing up, right in my face, screaming at me. Then I hear my own shaking, high-pitched voice – '*I'm sorry!*' He reaches over and grabs me, wrestling to push me to the ground.

I stop sniffling. 'You videoed it?'

Amber nods. 'Yes. We can take this to the police, or school. At the very least, he should get a warning for the things he said and did to you.'

I look up at Amber then – actually *look* at her for the first time in my life.

I never really thought of her like this. To be honest, I never really thought of her at all. She was always just that weird girl at the back of class. The person you forget is there.

I clear my throat.

'Thank you, um, Amber. For saving me. For everything.'

Two spots of pink have appeared on her cheeks. She looks away.

'It's fine, really,' she mumbles.

'I never – I guess we've never really spoken . . . At school, I mean,' I say.

Amber is staring at the ground. 'Oh yeah, I don't speak to many people, actually. It doesn't bother me. I don't need anyone. It's —'

But she doesn't seem able to finish her sentence. She avoids my gaze, but the evening sunlight catches her eyes, and I notice they're shining. Without thinking what I'm doing, I wrap both of my arms around her shoulders and pull her close towards me. The air rumbles with a chill, but the warmth of Amber's broad chest and shoulders stops me shivering.

I hug her tightly, and I feel her body relax against mine. I want to show how much her saving me meant, how much tension has left my body, how grateful I am for that video.

Amber lifts up her head, right next to mine, and I see tears are streaming down her cheeks.

'You shouldn't thank me. It's the least I could do after everything I've done to him,' she whispers.

'What do you mean? 'Everything *you've* done'?' I say.

Amber shakes her head. 'I'm just as bad.' She nods across to the distance. 'As him. Ren.'

I frown. 'Ren? Don't you mean Sven?'

Amber's brow is wrinkled. 'Sven? That's his Instagram handle, not his name. His real name is Ren Moore.'

I feel the colour drain out of my face.

Christ. *Could I have known any less about this guy?*

I shake my head, changing the subject. 'There's no way you're as bad as him. Whatever you've done.'

Amber keeps opening her mouth like she's on the brink of telling me something. Instinctively I link my arms in hers.

'He destroyed my life. He messaged the school, Louise, Tom. And thought he deserved me because he sent a few messages. You haven't done that to anyone.'

I can see snot dribbling down onto Amber's mouth. She wipes it away with her sleeve.

'I stalked him,' she says. 'Online. I knew everything about

229

him. The places he visited, who his best friends were. I even once turned up at his house. The only reason I knew he was here is because I saw his Snap Map location and followed him.'

She says this all so quickly, it's garbled.

'I thought I was doing something for him. But I wasn't. I was doing it for me. My whole life was checking him, watching him. I was obsessed. I . . .' Amber looks around, her eyes skimming the fields. 'I know exactly how Ren did this to you. How he got so angry with you. I didn't want to believe he did it. I – I would have done anything to believe him. I almost did.'

She blinks, hard, staring at the spot Sven was stood minutes earlier.

Amber shakes her head. 'I could have done the exact same thing.'

As she says the last bit, she stands up.

'I'm a freak. You don't have to tell me; I know it already.'

I stare at her for a moment.

It's like I'm really seeing her for the first time. For a second, I can almost imagine being Amber. Or even Sven. Having nothing in my life to focus on. Creating a fantasy, an obsession about someone I didn't know. I felt Sven's anger when he grabbed me, but I didn't understand it – it just seemed uncontrolled, mad.

Now there's also a twinge of sympathy. Imagine being Amber. Getting up every day, no one even noticing you're there, never speaking to anyone.

Stuck in your own head with your own thoughts.

*Every. Single. Day.*

'Sit down,' I say firmly.

Amber blinks at me. 'What?'

230

'Sit down, next to me. I wanna chat.'

I flop into a cross-legged position on the ground. Amber is eyeing me warily, like she thinks I'm about to bite.

'Honestly, I want to help you with this. You saved me from Sven. Sit down!' The strength in my voice is returning.

Amber folds her legs next to mine and settles on the grass.

I lean forward. 'You're not the same as him, for one. And do you know why?'

Amber shakes her head.

'Because you didn't do it. You didn't attack him, or call him names. You didn't act like he did.'

Amber is still staring at the ground. That's not the heart of the problem is it? That's not what this is really all about.

My voice softens. 'It doesn't come easily to you, does it. Speaking to people, making friends.'

Her face stiffens. 'No – but I don't need friends. I'm not—'

'Everyone needs friends,' I cut her off. 'They might not need to be loud. They might not like parties. They might want to spend ninety per cent of their time alone, doing their own thing, but everyone needs someone they can open up to – someone they can trust.'

My mind turns over my own relationships.

'I need Tom,' I say, only realizing the words are true once I hear them out loud. 'Louise and Ameerah, they're nice, they're fun to go out with, but I don't *need* them. I don't even need my mum, actually. But I need Tom.'

I think of that night I got with J, me veering round wildly at that party, flirting with everyone. 'I kind of go off the wall without him. He's my best friend; he makes me grounded. You might not need a boyfriend, or a girlfriend – but you need someone in your life. Someone you can be honest with, someone you can open up with.'

Amber blinks several times. 'But no one wants to be that person for me,' she says, so quietly I almost miss it. 'I can't . . . I can't get on with people like you can. I'm not pretty. I can't make them laugh. I don't understand it. I don't—'

Amber's face has contorted like she's thinking too hard.

I put a hand on her forearm. She looks up in surprise.

'Do you know how I do it?'

She blinks. 'How?'

'I don't think about it so much. Honestly, everyone is so fixed on themselves, no one is even thinking about what you're saying. No one even remembers. Just talk. If you say something weird, laugh at yourself. Say something else, everyone will have already forgotten.'

Amber half-smiles. 'It's easy for you. You're *Chloe MacNeil*.'

'And you're *Amber Nighy*. You just saved me from a guy that was twice your size, when you could have kept on walking. I don't know many people who would have done that.'

Amber's lower lip trembles. 'Thank you,' she says.

I lean forward and give her a tight hug.

# CHAPTER 52

## *Amber*

On the walk home, I can't stop thinking about what Chloe said. *'You saved me from a guy twice your size when you could have kept on walking. I don't know many people who would have done that.'*

The air has grown bitterly cold and is numbing my cheeks, but it's almost like I can't feel it. No one has ever said something like that to me before. Well, no one other than Mum or Dad.

Certainly not someone like Chloe MacNeil, the most popular girl in school.

For the first time, I'm starting to think maybe I'm not quite such a freak. Maybe the weird way I am isn't so bad . . . Maybe there are parts of me that are quite good too.

\*\*\*

When I get home, I stand in the hallway for a few seconds. Usually the first thing I would do is run up to my bedroom and pull out my laptop so I can start checking Ren's social media pages. But now I have absolutely zero desire to see what he's posted. It's almost like he's been scrubbed out of my mind – the thought of looking at his photos again just makes me cringe.

*How was I so naive?*

So I don't run upstairs. Instead, I rest my hand on the banister and listen. The muffled voices of Mum, Dad and Seb chatting in the living room echo through the hall. I pause for another moment and then slowly walk into the lounge.

Seb is standing up, pacing around the room, telling a loud story about something that happened to him and his friends at school. Mum laughs, and I can see the ghost of a smile playing on Dad's lips, though he's staring at the screen of his Kindle.

When I step in the room, Mum and Dad look up. Seb notices me and stops talking. He immediately comes bounding over, wrapping his arms around my shoulders.

'Y'all right, sis? Don't you need to go stalk people in your room?'

'Sebastian!' shouts Mum, frowning.

But I just roll my eyes at him, and then I go and sit between Mum and Dad on the sofa. I curl up my legs into the warmth, feeling like a small child again.

'You were right, Seb,' I say quietly.

'What?' he bellows. 'What did you say?'

'You were right about Ren.'

Mum's eyes snap with recognition, and she raises a hand to her head, groaning. 'Oh, Amber, please tell me you're not still stalking that poor boy . . .'

234

Seb snorts. 'He's not exactly a *poor boy*, Mum.'

My cheeks prickle with heat.

'Yeah, um, he's not. He tried to attack another girl. I saw him . . . um . . . with Chloe MacNeil.'

'Wait – what? You just saw Chloe MacNeil?' says Seb.

He immediately wheels on me and starts asking a million questions a second. Rather than shrinking away from him, I instead pluck at a thread on my jumper and quietly tell him, Mum and Dad exactly what happened.

I tell them about finding Ren and Chloe on a date together. That I heard her scream, and he tried to pin her to the ground. That I . . .

I pause for breath at that point. Mum's eyes have grown wide, and even Dad has pushed his glasses to the end of his nose and is looking right at me. He opens his mouth, and Seb cuts in, laughing.

'And then a guy came over, scared him off, right?'

I shake my head. 'No. That's not what happened. I shouted at him. I scared him off.'

'You – what?'

'*I* scared him off.'

All of my family are looking at me like I've grown an extra head. But then Dad gives a snort.

'Well sounds like good riddance,' he says, giving me a small smile before he goes back to reading his Kindle.

Mum is looking at me agog. 'You shouldn't have done that – you should have called for help,' she says, and then starts giving me a lecture on safety.

I nod, and try to look like I agree, but when I glance up,

I can see Seb's face behind Mum and Dad, on the far sofa, grinning at me.

***

Twenty minutes later, me and Seb have retired to his bedroom. I'm sitting on the edge of his bed, playing with the same delicate thread on the hem of my jumper. He's pacing around the floor, throwing a tennis ball up and gently bouncing it off the ceiling.

'Christ,' says Seb, after a while. 'You saved Chloe MacNeil from Ren. He's a built guy.'

There's a note of admiration in his voice. When I look up, he's staring at me with his head tilted to one side.

'I know –' he clears his throat – 'you guys aren't friends, but you . . . you did that, for Chloe—'

It sounds like a question.

I shrug. 'No. She's not my friend, but I'm not going to let her get hurt.'

Seb is still looking at me. The tennis ball falls with a thud somewhere between us.

'I dunno, he was a dick to all those girls, and no one really said anything. Or did anything. It's just . . . pretty cool, what you did.'

I furrow my brow. 'Pretty cool?'

'Yep.' Seb's eyes crinkle. 'Now don't make me say it again.'

I twist the thread of fabric round and round my thumb, and I smile.

# CHAPTER 53

# *Amber*

On Monday morning, I'm walking towards the humanities block before school starts, on my way to meet Chloe. We've been messaging ever since Saturday, but somehow it doesn't feel like all the messages I've got before. They haven't made me dizzyingly pleased, or worried about how to reply. They just make me feel . . . happy.

I keep fidgeting on my way to the school. Part of me can't really believe that Chloe doesn't mind being seen with me. Won't it make her look worse, somehow, that she is hanging out with me? Won't it make her popularity crash by about a million points?

It's the same hot, prickling feeling I get when Seb wants to speak to me at school. I know he doesn't actually want to speak to me, not really, so how can I minimize myself enough that I won't make him look bad?

Despite the cold, the sun is breaking through the clouds, and I can feel a warm tickle across my cheeks. I see Chloe standing there at the front of school looking utterly radiant, even though it's only 7 a.m., her clear cheeks and glossy hair shining as she beams at me.

'Hey,' she says with a confidence I could never fake, smiling at me.

'Hey,' I whisper back.

But Chloe doesn't give me time to think, she launches into talking a mile a minute about our plan.

She's got a meeting before school this morning with Ms Benewood, to 'reintroduce' her after her suspension, but Chloe wants to confront her. Well, she wants *us* to confront her. Show her the video of Ren. Get her to apologize.

After Chloe has finished talking, she glances at me, her eyes sharp. 'Does that work for you?'

'Yes,' I say, feeling my mouth turn dry.

What I don't understand is how Chloe can do this – be so confident, while I'm so quiet. And yet when Ren was there, attacking us, she broke down, and *I* was the one who had the strength to fight back.

Right now, it feels like the last thing I could do. But when Chloe glances back and smiles at me, I begin to feel like I can.

***

Fifteen minutes later, we're both sitting across from Ms Benewood at her desk, and Chloe is explaining everything.

Ms Benewood leans back in her chair. She's got her arms folded across her chest and raises an eyebrow as Chloe recounts her theory.

Before she speaks, Ms Benewood glances at me with one eye.

Ms Benewood sighs. 'The thing is, girls, that I just can't see how this could have happened. All right, you know he followed you on social media, but we've had no reports of someone hacking your emails, Chloe. No unauthorized sign ins.'

This is my cue. 'He wouldn't have had to sign in—' I interrupt, my mind ticking over all the things I found (and almost used) when I was tracking Ren.

Ms Benewood blinks. 'Excuse me?'

'Chloe, you never found the sent emails, did you?'

Chloe shakes her head.

'Well, then,' I go on, 'he could have used a ghosting program, where they look like they're sent from your email. All he would need to know is the email address, or the format of our email addresses – which he could have guessed from the school website.'

Ms Benewood is still looking at both of us levelly. 'How would he have gotten those photos of Louise? Girls, I understand this desire to prove your innocence, but honestly I do think this is a little elaborate—'

'We don't know about the photos—' I start.

'Show her the video,' cuts in Chloe, nodding to my phone.

My mouth turns dry. 'A-are you sure?'

Chloe's teeth are set. 'Yes. It's the only way. Show her.'

I turn and spin my phone towards Ms Benewood, while Chloe starts slowly explaining how she decided to confront Ren.

As Ms Benewood watches the video, her face changes from a mixture of disbelief to horror.

There's a long pause after the video finishes, and she shuffles uncomfortably in her chair.

Chloe is looking straight at Ms Benewood, her big green eyes piercingly steady.

Ms Benewood eventually clears her throat.

'I think we need to phone the police.'

# CHAPTER 54

## Chloe

By the time I walk into the Year Eleven block, I know the news will have already swept through school. This morning, I posted a long Facebook post about 'my experience with a cyberstalker' and even attached a snippet of the video from Amber's phone, which I put together over the weekend. The post has already got 113 likes and more than twenty comments.

Before registration, I can hear the clipping of Louise's heeled shoes on the laminate floor before I see her. The girls are all back around me, and I laugh loudly at something Ameerah's just said. I'm about to pretend I haven't seen Louise – make her seek me out – but then I shake myself.

No. She's your friend. Don't make this more difficult for her.

I turn my head and catch her eye. Louise's cheeks are puce, but she lifts her chin slightly.

'Chloe. C-c-can I have a word?'

All the other girls are staring at her. In fact, I think the whole class queuing outside our form room is.

I shrug. 'Sure.'

***

Once it's just us two, standing in one of the small music rooms further along the corridor, Louise takes a deep breath.

'I-I —' She stops, clears her throat, and then starts again. 'I had no idea . . .' she says, so quietly it's almost a whisper. 'I thought . . . you and Jerome – I thought—'

I stand there, watching her.

'I'm so sorry. I didn't mean—' Her eyes are starting to fill with tears. She tries to dab them with her sleeve so they don't spill mascara down her cheeks.

I sigh. It's the first time I've made a noise since Louise started speaking, and she looks up, startled.

'How did he get those photos?' I say quietly.

Louise is snivelling now, sniffing into her sleeve. Her lips are trembling. 'I sent them,' she whispers.

'What? You sent them to Sven?'

'No, no! I got a message from someone I thought was Jerome. He said he'd got locked out of Instagram and was using a new account, and could I resend him the pictures I'd sent the other night as they'd been wiped.'

'And you didn't tell me?'

'I'm sorry! I sent them and then felt so stupid. I didn't think. And then when they got emailed out, I just assumed . . . I don't know . . . It didn't feel right.' She sniffs. 'I should have believed you.'

242

'It's OK,' I say.

Louise blinks. 'Serious?'

I shake my head. 'Yes. He was a freak. I thought something weird was going on too. I should have mentioned it to you but –' I sigh – 'I was embarrassed. I didn't want to tell you.'

'It's so awful.' Louise starts gabbling. 'What happened to you – I can't believe it! You shouldn't have had to put up with that! What did he do when you saw him? I saw a bit of the video clip, but that's only a few seconds. What—'

I cut Louise off. 'The photos coming out, what happened to you – it's awful too!'

I lean forward and give her tall frame a big hug. She squeezes me hard back.

Pulling away, I hold her at arm's length. 'I'll tell all of you what happened together – c'mon.'

Louise stays put. 'I really am sorry,' she says, so softly I almost can't hear her.

I link my arm in hers. 'Me too.'

\*\*\*

When we walk back into class, I spot Amber sitting right at the back, her head down, staring at the desk. If I'm honest, it's the first time I've seen her in registration, and if I wasn't looking for her, I probably wouldn't even notice she was there.

The girls all gather around me as soon as I sit down, leaning in, asking for details. The boys too start shouting things at me about being 'wronged'. I smile and flick my hair over one shoulder.

Everything is back how it used to be, but that's not how I want it to be.

Ms Brown is standing at the front of class now, peering over her spectacles as she tries to call out the register.

No one is listening; they're all focused on me.

Everyone is whispering, asking questions. The girls sitting on desks either side have twisted their chairs so they are directly facing me. A couple of the guys have actually left their seats and are perched on the desk closest to me, waving and trying to get my attention.

I look across at Amber.

*She's the furthest from me she possibly could be. She's* the one who saved *me* from Sven – I mean, Ren. And she's the only person in class who doesn't have someone sitting next to her.

Ms Brown starts shouting at the boys to get back to their seats.

Abruptly I stand up.

'Ms Brown?' I call out.

She blinks. 'What is it, Chloe?'

'I was wondering if I could say a few words about what happened with my cyberstalker to the whole class.'

A murmur sweeps across the room. I can feel everyone's eyes on me.

'G'on, miss! Let her say,' shouts one of the guys from the back.

Ms Brown shushes him. 'I think that would be an excellent idea. In fact, we can dedicate a PSHE lesson to cyberstalking, but right now might not be the best ti—'

'Thank you, Ms Brown,' I say, waving my hand at her.

I push back my seat noisily and go to stand at the front of

the class. She doesn't stop me. Every single eye is on me. I can feel myself warming up, coming alive under their gaze.

At the very back, Amber's head lifts.

I clear my throat. 'As you all know, I had a stalker.' A hushed, excited whisper goes out across the entire class. 'A cyberstalker. He ghosted my email, my social media accounts, my . . . well, my whole life. He fooled everyone.'

Louise's cheeks flush pink.

'So I decided to meet him.'

There's a gasp from someone at the back of class.

'Which I know now was a terrible idea.'

The class is deathly silent, rapt with attention. Slowly, I start explaining what happened. How he seemed normal, he seemed OK – at first. I talked about how angry I got with his messages, how he started to turn.

Then I lower my voice and talk about how I felt. How scared I was – how I didn't realize how stupid it was to think I could know someone I'd never met.

'I should never have gone to meet him. He wasn't who I thought he was, he was dangerous. I felt powerless, scared.'

Amber is staring straight at me. I put my hand on my hip.

'But there's one person in this room who intervened. Who stopped him.'

A few eyes swivel to Ameerah, Louise – my other girls – but I ever so slightly shake my head.

'This girl came up behind him when he had me pinned to the ground. She scared him – got him off me. He was like, six foot something and massive, but she stopped him.' I lower my voice. 'I don't know what would have happened if Amber Nighy hadn't been walking past that day.'

245

There's another gasp from somewhere in the class. Then one of the guys scoffs.

'Amber Nighy? What the hell was *she* doing there?'

I look straight at him, and he shuts up.

'She shouted at him. She stopped the stalker.'

No one is staring at me any more. They've all turned round to look at Amber – who is slowly turning bright red.

Ms Brown steps forward. 'I think what this calls for is a round of applause – for both of you.'

I can feel myself cringe. Oh God! Why do teachers always do this? Why did she have to make things so lame?

But as Ms Brown claps as loudly as a brass brand, the others start joining in. There's a wolf whistle from one of the guys, then he claps Amber on the back of the shoulder.

'Well done, Nighy!'

'Yeah, thanks, Amber,' says Louise.

As the class applauds, I walk back to my seat and catch Amber's eye. She looks mortified as people shout things at her, but when she sees me, I wave.

And she gives a tiny smile back.

# CHAPTER 55

# *Amber*

It feels like I've stepped into a parallel universe. Normally I feel invisible at school, but today, it's like a spotlight has been shone on every inch of me. All of me is illuminated: nothing is in the dark.

But it also feels like I'm under hot lights. My cheeks have been on fire ever since Chloe stood up and talked about me in registration. I've managed to steal away into the corridor now, but after class, everyone kept coming up to me, clapping me on the back, asking me questions about what happened.

People who last week wouldn't even have looked at me if I'd tried to speak to them.

I'd always expected being the centre of attention to feel great. I thought it must be wonderful to be like Seb and have everyone wanting to talk to you, but for some reason, I don't feel ecstatic. Instead I just feel . . . awkward.

People keep wanting to know more and more. I've had to repeat the same story again and again. How I fended off Ren;

how I 'saved' Chloe. And I've had to skirt the questions about why I was there in the first place.

Chloe hasn't mentioned what I confided in her about stalking Ren. When she describes the story, it's like I came out of nowhere to save her. She makes it funny, too. She came over earlier while people were asking me questions, and I was stuttering, and immediately took over the conversation, while somehow still making everyone stare at me in wonder.

She knows how to tell a story, Chloe. Not only that, but she knows how to make people like her. How to be the centre of attention without blushing and wishing the floor would swallow her up. In fact, she seems to come alive when everyone is watching.

We couldn't be more different.

As I'm walking along now with the final bell ringing, I catch several people's eyes, but immediately look down so they don't try to come over. When I look back up, a couple of people are still glancing at me as they put on their coats, but I stare rigidly at the floor until they stop.

My feet are walking faster and faster without me paying attention. As I wander across the school playground, I can feel the eyes on me melting away either side. I find myself heading towards a familiar, quieter place.

My steps slowly curve in the direction of the gym.

My stomach twinges as I think of the last time I was here, the last time I saw him.

When I get to the wall where he always stood, there's no one there. Just an empty space. I guess it is past five o'clock.

I pull my jumper low over my fingertips. Then – without

248

thinking about what I'm doing – I push open the door and step through into the warm.

There's a figure directly in front of me, and as soon as I see their face, they smile.

'Hey,' I say, in a quieter voice than I was expecting.

Iulia beams at me and comes over.

# CHAPTER 56

# *Chloe*

Mum doesn't believe me until the school rings up on Monday night, mainly because I haven't bothered telling her what happened. She listens intently for several moments, saying 'uh-huh, uh-huh', and occasionally interrupting them in a sharp voice to ask questions.

I'm sitting on the sofa in a big, soft jumper and woolly socks, with a notebook propped up on my lap, sketching the shape of our cat Jemima, who is curled up next to me, when Mum marches into the living room.

'You had a stalker?!' she says, with a mixture of horror and excitement. 'Oh-my-God! Darling!' She rushes over and her slimy skin – slathered in expensive-smelling moisturizer – clasps my hand.

'I can't *believe* how wronged you were! Just wait until I tell Tallie about this!' she exclaims, rushing back to the kitchen to pick up her phone.

I stare after her for a few moments.

That was it? '*I can't believe how wronged you were*' and '*Just wait until I tell Tallie about this?*' No apology for not believing me. No real interest in the situation, apart from that it's a titbit of drama to gossip about with her stupid friend. To be honest, I didn't really expect her to be that invested. Or apologize, even.

Meanwhile, my own phone is filling up with messages. Buzzing every few seconds as the news sweeps across school.

> **Rachel** I never doubted you!

> **Ameerah** I can't believe what he did! What a psycho.

There's also a message from Tom.

> **Tom** You went to see him, and you didn't tell me?! Call me!

My heart is heavy as I read his message. I know I should call Tom – but ever since I told Amber that I need him, I've been feeling . . . I don't know. Scared. Scared to tell him about seeing Sve— I mean, Ren. Scared to admit I did it without telling him. Scared to admit how much danger I put myself in.

At that moment, my phone lights up with another WhatsApp message. I drop my notebook onto Jemima's tail.

> **Louise** Do you want to come over
> this weekend?

I stare down at it. I'm almost tempted to say no, as I'm already going over to Ameerah's. But something has changed. I think of Amber, spending every single day at school alone . . . the things I said. I think about Tom – how much I argued with him, made him suffer, for stupid reasons.

I shake my head. I don't want to be that person. I start typing.

> **Chloe** Sure! I was planning to go to
> Ameerah's. Come with? x

Then I click open Tom's chat icon.

> **Chloe** Can we speak in person?
> After lessons? I'll be in tomorrow.

And finally, I tap in Amber's number and type out a message to her.

> **Chloe** Hey, how are you doing? We
> should catch up sometime at school!

Then I let my phone drop to my lap, pick up my notebook, and go back to sketching a fluffy, annoyed-looking Jemima.

# CHAPTER 57

## *Amber*

Somehow, even Iulia has heard about me confronting Ren. It must have been from one of the school PE groups that come in to the gym during the day. And she can't stop talking about it. Her eyes are shining, and her cheeks are flushed as she asks me question after question.

I tell her everything, feeling my voice stutter when she gasps at moments in the story. After I've finished explaining what happened, Iulia raises her eyebrows at me.

'You showed him, girl,' she says, whistling.

I smile at her. Even with just one person, the attention is making me uncomfortable. But there's something else I want to ask her. Something I can't quite understand.

'Iulia . . .' I pause, not quite sure how to phrase this. 'When you told me your story, about Ren, about how you met. Well . . . you mentioned you met in September. But I remember hearing that the course starts in October.'

I glance up.

Iulia looks nonplussed. She tilts her head to one side and wrinkles her nose.

'Yes, the course starts in October, but we met at an open day over the summer, then we started gyming together all of September.'

She says this so casually, like it's nothing.

'Ah, that makes sense,' I say.

She grins. 'What? Did you think I was lying?'

She looks so incredulous that I find myself laughing back.

I think of Jemma – that Instagram photo that Ansh posted, the one I thought made her story unbelievable. Then I think of Maisie – how I never found out her side of the story. How I was convinced that not speaking to her meant it didn't happen.

So what if Ansh posted a photo the same night Jemma said she was with Ren? Maybe she got her dates muddled. Maybe Ren asked him to post it as a cover-up.

All those hours and hours I spent looking at his social media profiles, looking for clues. They weren't clues, were they? They were a carefully curated profile that he wanted everyone to see.

It's like looking for blemishes on an airbrushed magazine. Completely and utterly pointless.

I stare at the wall for a few seconds.

'So, what do you want to work on today? What were your goals again?' says Iulia, with a smile.

I blink at her. I never even thought about my fitness goals. Every trip I've had to the gym so far has been about Ren. Either hoping to bump into him or wanting to speak to Ansh or Iulia so I could quiz them about him getting fired.

Now that's gone, and I'm standing here in the gym without

my face flushing, my stomach clenching with nerves, it feels . . . oddly freeing.

I look round at all the machines I've never bothered to learn the names of. I could spend lunchtime running, or jogging, or rowing.

I look back at Iulia, and I smile.

'What do you suggest?'

# CHAPTER 58

# *Chloe*

The next morning before registration, Tom is waiting for me by my locker. My stomach does a weird somersault when I see him. He doesn't look how he usually does – his hair is slightly rumpled, and he has deep purple rings under his eyes. When he sees me, he doesn't even say hello, just steps forward, his mouth open.

'What the hell?! What were you thinking – going and seeing that stalker all by yourself? Why didn't you *tell* me! I would have come with you.'

He looks pissed off. I can feel my body shrinking away, wanting to turn and run. Or shout at him, tell him it's not working, before bolting, like I would have done before. But I shake my head.

*No.*

He's not being unfair, is he? I should have told him what I was doing. I *was* stupid. If Amber hadn't been there . . . well, then anything could have happened.

I bite my lip. 'I'm sorry.'

He looks shocked, like I've blown the wind out of his sails.

'You're right. I should have told you. I shouldn't have done it. I shouldn't have put myself in danger.'

Tom's face almost instantly softens. He looks at me for a second, then puts his head in his hands.

'How do you think I felt when I heard? What if that other guy hadn't come and stopped it? What if you'd just been left—'

'It wasn't another guy.'

'What?'

'The person who scared him away. It wasn't another guy. It was Amber Nighy – she's in my form.'

Tom looks completely blank. 'Oh, right. I don't think I know her.'

'She's really cool,' I say, lifting my chin up.

Tom frowns. 'OK, great. So you got lucky. That doesn't make it better. I should have come with you.'

Anger starts burning through me, but when I look at Tom's frowning face, the fire dampens. He's only annoyed because he *cares*. This is someone the opposite of Mum. Someone who's actually got my back.

'I promise I won't do anything like this again,' I say.

Tom sighs. 'You're not going to meet up with any more stalkers without telling me, right?'

I look up and see the sides of his mouth are twitching.

'Hmm?'

'Fine. No more stalkers,' I say, almost smiling. 'But I don't need to tell you where I am. I can go wherever I want.'

Tom shakes his head. 'I know that. Christ. Why do I put up with you?'

I wrap my arms around his warm body, and he drops a kiss on the top of my head.

'I'm sorry,' I mumble.

He doesn't say anything else. I push my head up, and he leans down to kiss me.

As our lips meet, the warmth of his skin slows my pulse.

The weight of the last month seems to melt away. The frenzied late-night messages between me and Sven, or Ren, or whoever the hell he was. That drunk night. The desperate, relentless desire for attention. J grabbing my breast. The constant feeling of unease sat deep in the pit of my stomach.

But now, with Tom, I don't feel scared, or unsettled, or manic.

I just feel right.

# CHAPTER 59

## Amber

After thirty minutes on the rowing machine, I've worked up such a sweat that I'm incredibly thankful there are showers at the gym. I step out into the chill of the evening air, with a few tendrils of damp hair flapping around my face.

For the first time since I can remember, my thoughts are still.

My mind isn't electrified, stuck on a loop thinking about Ren, imagining how he feels, itching to check his social media. I can feel my hair damp against the nape of my neck, the wind slapping my cheeks, and the rising sound of chatter coming from the nearby playground – and it makes me smile.

As I'm looking out over the leisure centre car park, I see him.

He makes me stop dead in my tracks. He's standing by the edge of the gym, one foot up against the wall, staring down at his phone.

I genuinely haven't thought about him all day, yet here he is, standing mere metres away from me. And he hasn't seen me. He doesn't know I'm here – not yet. It feels weird looking at someone in real life when they don't know you're there.

So I don't. I take a deep breath and take a few steps towards him. He looks up, and his dark hair twitches across his cheeks in the wind.

'Hey,' I say, so quietly I'm not sure he can even hear me.

Ansh doesn't respond; he just glances back down at his phone. I think he's going to ignore me completely, but then after a couple of seconds he says, 'Hey.'

I bite my lip. 'I was just . . . um – I wanted to say . . .'

How is it possible that I can shout at Ren like that, yet I don't have the nerve to apologize to Ansh without stuttering?

I furrow my brow. 'I'm – I'm sorry.'

Ansh looks up and frowns. 'Why are you sorry?' he says, his voice gruff.

'For lying. For saying I was Ren's sister. I didn't go on a date with him either; that was another lie. I just . . . I don't know – I behaved like a freak. I just wanted to find out what was going on with him. When I heard about him getting fired, I got carried away. I lied because I wanted to find out . . .' I take a deep breath. 'Just – for *everything*, I'm sorry.'

Ansh's expression has changed slightly, and he's looking at me with his lips apart. 'It's fine.' He rubs his temples. 'OK, I guess I was a bit annoyed. Particularly when you lied about being his sister. I mean . . . who *does* that?'

My whole body cringes. 'Oh God. I *know*.'

'Then you told Iulia you were dating him!' says Ansh, his voice rising slightly.

'Don't!' I can feel heat spreading over my body, climbing up my cheeks. I put my hands over my eyes and groan.

264

When I slowly uncover my eyes, Ansh isn't backing away from me with a scared expression like I'm this huge, socially inept freak. Instead, he's laughing.

'A tip: next time, if you want to do some subtle investigative work, don't make out you're dating your brother!'

'Aargh.' I cringe inwardly. 'I really am sorry.'

He shrugs, smiling. 'Nah. It's cool.'

At that moment, Iulia comes bounding out of the gym with a big smile.

'Oh hey, you two!' she says, her wavy red hair bouncing either side of her face. 'Were you talking about Amber videoing Ren?'

Ansh's eyebrows shoot up to his hairline. 'You what?'

'No, no, no – it wasn't. It was —'

I catch both of their eyes then and suddenly, like a spark between us, we all immediately start laughing.

Iulia is giggling the loudest. 'Not like *that*! She saved Chloe MacNeil – you know the one. Loud, dark hair . . .'

Iulia launches into the story again, and my cheeks threaten to flush, but somehow I meet both of their eyes.

'Christ. Did you *hit* him? He's a big guy,' says Ansh.

'No, I didn't hit anyone. I shouted at him – told him to get off Chloe.'

Ansh bursts out laughing again. 'I can't believe you actually scared him off. I mean, there's probably not a person alive who deserves it more, but that's priceless.'

Iulia is grinning too, her cheeks shining with freckles. 'We know not to mess with Amber,' she says.

I look at them both now, a warmth spreading through me. I remember Iulia bounding over at the garden centre, helping me with my fitness. Ansh sending me those funny GIFs, even though he didn't have to. Them both standing here now, actually taking the time to speak to me, laughing *with* me.

Then I think of Ren's smile. The ghost of a gesture: fleeting, superficial.

Every lunchtime for the last six months, I've sat alone for an hour by myself. I think of what Chloe said about me to everyone – how she made me visible. The hundreds of people today who crowded round me, wanting to hear my story. How it just made me want to hide.

But being here, with Iulia and Ansh, I don't want to disappear. I want to stay right where I am.

Whenever I meet Ansh or Iulia's eyes, they don't send a shiver down my spine like Ren's did. But they make me feel warm, like Mum, Dad and Seb. Like I'm an actual person worth speaking to.

I clear my throat. 'Do you . . . um – this is probably dumb – but do you two fancy grabbing something to eat tomorrow lunch?'

I can imagine being at school, leaving morning lessons like everyone else. Watching Seb run over to his band of mates, hearing the chatter and laughter all around me. Having my own place to go and people to speak to. Maybe Ansh and Iulia won't be my people, but then again . . . who knows?

Ansh looks down at me, and his eyes crinkle. 'Yeah, sure.'

Beside him, Iulia nods ferociously.

I smile shyly back.

Ansh squints down at me, his eyes half closed. I look away, a flush warming my cheeks.

We might not get on. Maybe we'll argue the entire time, or only go for lunch once and then never speak again.

They might be completely different to how I expect.
But this time, I'm not going to imagine.
I'm going to find out for real.

## THE END

# ABOUT THE AUTHOR

Charlotte Seager lives in London with her partner David and her cat Ruby. She grew up in the Suffolk countryside and moved to London after university to join *the Guardian* as a writer on the children's books site. She went on to be editor of the Guardian Careers desk, before moving papers earlier this year to join *The Times and The Sunday Times* as engagement editor, building online communities.

# ACKNOWLEDGMENTS

My mum, my best friend, thank you for being with me every step of the way – you know how much your love and friendship means to me.

My husband David, I couldn't do half the things I've achieved in life without your never-ending love and support – every day with you is an adventure, thank you.

My Dad, you have taught me a quiet resilience and rebelliousness which helped me to keep writing whenever I faltered, thank you.

My brothers, James and George, the inspiration behind Seb and Aidy (you always manage to feature in one of my books!) thank you.

A huge thank you to my brilliant editors Simran and Rachel: the story has transformed with your edits, and is so, so much better as a result! And thank you to the whole Macmillan team, it has been an absolute pleasure to work with you all on my second book, your enthusiasm and expertise has really brought the story to life.

Thank you to my agent Annette Green, for championing my writing from the very beginning.

And finally thank you to you for reading my book. I never imagined anyone would read the stories I write, the very best part of writing is hearing from readers.

I'm delighted that you found this story.

Thank you.
Love, Charlotte x

Turn the page for an exciting extract
from Charlotte Seager's first novel . . .

*I just want you to know I never wanted to do this.*

*I never wanted to ruin your life.*

*You need to know that what is about to happen isn't my fault. If you hadn't done what you did, there wouldn't be anything to ruin. If you hadn't lied to us – all 3,054,263 of us.*

*I trusted you so, so much. I trusted everything you said, everything you told us. How could I have been so stupid?*

*You deserve all that's going to happen to you. But it also hurts to think of what you're going to go through – the paparazzi, the abuse, the trolls.*

*I want you to know that I feel bad for doing this, even though it's your own fault. I don't want to hurt you, but I need to make sure people know the truth – one person in particular. Even if you're not who I thought you were, surely even you understand that I have no choice. It's the most important thing I have ever done.*

*In ten seconds' time I'm going to click publish. Then everyone will know the truth. Everyone will know you lied to us all.*

*But I wanted to write to you first, just to say I'm sorry.*

*Issa x*

1

# ONE MONTH
# EARLIER

# CHAPTER 1

I can't even imagine three million people.

I can imagine ten people lined up in a queue. Or about a hundred – Bryan's gigs often hold several hundred faces – but any more and it starts to go fuzzy. How many people can fit in the largest stadium in the world – fifty thousand? A hundred thousand, maybe?

I imagine rows upon rows of seats filled up with faces. Each face a whole life's worth of experiences, families and relationships. Nope. I can't picture it. Even a hundred thousand is unthinkable.

3,002,031

A wave of panic washes over me.

On a day-to-day basis, I don't think about how many people are watching me. But when I do it doesn't feel real. My stomach twists with a mingling of excitement and fear. I can't believe I've hit three million. This is really, properly huge. This is insane.

Instinctively I reach for my camera. What is Bryan going to say? We've been talking about hitting three million for months. The numbers have been creeping closer and closer. I can't wait to tell him!

I lean over to the mirror to check my face. Ugh, I look disgusting. I haven't been thinking about filming all day. Smoothing down my hair, I slick on some lip salve and pull a face at the camera – oh, screw it. I've looked worse. The viewfinder needs adjusting to get my face in shot, and . . . record.

'Bryan! I've hit three million subscribers!'

It feels strange saying the number out loud. Three million people watch your videos. Three million people know who you are. Three million.

Nothing.

'Bryan! I've hit three million!' I say again.

Huh, where is he? The corridor is empty, but there's a faint buzzing of electricity coming from the room at the far end. I go in and see him crouched over his electric guitar, with his phone on his lap, smirking at the screen.

OK, I'm going to scare him. This will make a great shot. I press my fingers to my lips and mouth 'Shh' at the camera. Then I point the camera at my feet and do exaggerated tiptoes behind him.

'I'VE HIT THREE MILLION!' I yell in his ear.

Bryan leaps out of his skin and spins the laptop away from me. He pulls off his headphones.

'Lily, what the hell?!'

His loose hoody has fallen off his shoulder, revealing a long grey tank top – the feathered edge of his black raven tattoo peeping over his shoulder. His fingers, calloused by guitar

4

strings, clink with rings as he throws his phone across the desk.

I stare at him, the sound of the phone clattering between us. His dilated pupils flick from me to the lens, and he finally twigs.

Great, he knows I'll have to edit that out.

'Err . . . you hit three million? Oh, no way – congrats.'

He gets up and envelopes me in a hug. I stay frigid at first, irritated with him. But then he clutches me tighter and I nuzzle into his scratchy beard and hard, skinny chest – my arm moving round us to get the shot.

My heart starts to thud as I think of all my subscribers – all their imaginary faces swimming in front of me. It almost feels like too many people to please. Too much to deal with.

'I-I just can't believe it,' I mumble thickly, feeling my vision blur.

Bryan whispers into my hair, away from the mic. 'I mean, that is a lot of pre-teen stalkers.'

He sees my face, and changes tack.

'You know what, let's get brunch to celebrate,' he says loudly, stretching his lips goofily at the camera.

I smile. I'm already thinking how I can edit this into a full vlog. We'll need some footage of us getting brunch, perhaps an Instagram if I can get a good shot of the food . . . then if we could get something of us thanking the viewers, perhaps wandering around a park. That would look good. Or did we do a park last week? I could end it with a monologue into the camera saying how grateful I am.

My chest feels tight. I've got two sponsored videos to finish by the end of today, and I'm only halfway through the emails my PA Sam has sent over. I also really should do an Instagram post. But that last shot should be pretty easy to film. If I can get enough footage of us at the breakfast place, I can fill most of the vlog with me talking after I've finished my work. It'll need editing though, but I can do that tonight. My mind starts whirling with things to do. I put a hand on my neck and feel my blood pulsing against my fingertips.

I can't not upload a vlog tomorrow when I've hit three million. Maybe if I get up at six tomorrow, I can fit in the editing. It won't take long, anyway. I won't film much, and it'll be under ten minutes – I'll try to keep my filming to about forty. I'll just have to fit it in, somehow.

Ouch. I flinch and realize I've bitten my lip so hard it's bleeding. Shit. I'll have to edit that out. I look up at Bryan.

'That would be amazing!' I smile, twinkling my eyes at the lens and reaching past Bry to place the camera on the desk.

Bryan's phone starts buzzing, and he reaches across me to retrieve it. When his eyes catch the screen, he smirks. 'I, um, just need to finish up on some music stuff.' He smiles at me and nods to the door. 'Be ready in ten.'

# CHAPTER 2

## Melissa

I wish I looked like LilyLoves. She's just posted a selfie on Instagram to celebrate hitting three million – and she looks amazing. She has these huge eyes, framed thickly by smoky black kohl liner and long sweeping lashes. Her hair is also perfect – in a pixie cut, which she styles into these beautiful blonde wisps that skim her eyes.

I could never pull off short hair; my face is way too fat. And my hair is the same dull mousey-brown colour as Mum's – I would look like a boy. Not a cute, girly-looking boy either. An actual boy. People at school would go, 'Hey, who's the new guy in form H?' And when I'd sit next to Suze she would probably go bright red and refuse to speak to me.

She's like that with boys.

I click on Lily's latest post – 'A Little London Adventure' – and scroll through the photos. She's clutching a pot of strawberries outside a market stall, her fingers bejewelled with rough amethyst and topaz rings. *Had a wonderful day exploring London with my lovely friend – hope your weekend was also fabulous! Love Lily xoxox*

I love Lily's blogs. Every time I see a place she's visited, it makes me desperate to go there. When she posts a breakfast Instagram, it looks so good I just want to reach through the screen and devour it.

Actually, it's probably a good thing I can't. I'm already a bit chubby around my thighs. If I ate like Lily, I would probably need a crane to lift me into school. There's a picture of her crouched over a beanbag in leggings – these long silver beaded necklaces draped across her chest. My legs will never be that tiny.

I tried to re-create that picture a few weeks ago, but the only necklaces I have are these cheap silver ones from H&M, which I've worn so much the colour has faded. I tried stealing a couple of Mum's gold necklaces, but when she saw me taking photos she didn't understand and freaked out.

'What are you doing wearing my necklaces and photographing yourself? This isn't for the internet, is it? Melissa, tell me you're not posting that to THE INTERNET!'

She says I-N-T-E-R-N-E-T like it's this scary place where paedophiles go to lure children away. I bet she has no idea that the girls from school use it to trick boys into saying they like them on messenger, before screenshotting what they say and sending it to the entire class. There's no point even trying to explain vlogging to her.

It was pointless anyway – the selfies looked terrible. I don't have the bone structure.

As I'm scrolling through Lily's feed, I open another tab and click on Bryan's YouTube page. I don't find Bryan's channel half as fun; he mainly just talks about weird music. I tap through to his Instagram page. I mean, I don't mind the photos of his

8

bandmate Jerry – he's quite hot – but my favourite thing is the pictures he posts of him and Lily.

Before long, I find what I'm looking for – a selfie of Bryan and Lily snuggled up on the sofa together with Bryan's parents' little white puppy, Polar, wriggling between them. Bry's pulling a mock stern face, Polar's paws are entwined in his beard, while Lily has her head tipped back with an easy smile.

They look so happy. I click through to Lily's vlog channel, LilyLives, and open a video of them exploring London. These are my favourite. Bry is running ahead, laughing and jumping on some railings, while Lily is pretending not to watch and rolling her eyes.

'Seriously, Lily, what is this – 2005? Let's order it online,' he complains as she drags him into a supermarket. Then Lily pouts, and he laughs, spinning his feet round to follow her.

I lose a good hour wrapped up in their videos, in fact it's 12 p.m. before I notice the time. Oh crap. Mum, Dad and my brother, Aidy, will be back from swimming soon. I tear myself away from Lily's videos and look around my room. Mum is going to flip. It's a mess of clothes, hairbrushes and discarded make-up. My life is so much worse than Lily's – I wish I had a beautiful home and a boyfriend.

Not that Bryan is really my type – there are much better-looking guys in lower sixth. Bry is very skinny, and his eyes are slightly too close together. But then he does have the whole band thing, which somehow makes him sexier. And he does really care for Lily.

Nibbling my nail, I think about what life would be like if I had a boyfriend. Me and a tall, dark, good-looking guy going for a trip to London – posting pictures on my blog of us visiting quirky restaurants, coming back to our flat to rustle up dinner, him laughing and teaching me to cook. Or maybe we'd both be terrible at cooking, so we'd get a takeaway and snuggle up together, kissing the grease off each other's lips . . .

I click back to Lily's blog. The pathetic thing is I don't have a boyfriend. I haven't even kissed a boy. Well, not properly. I had a couple of awkward lip clashes with my boyfriend Yousef a couple of years ago, but we were such little kids – it wasn't a real relationship. At the end of year nine, he moved schools, so I dumped him. That was the depth of our love.

Sixteen years old and I've never had a proper boyfriend. This is my life.

I open my own blog and split the screen so it's side by side with Lily's. All I've written about so far is make-up reviews, and I've now exhausted everything in my collection. My follower count is stubbornly stuck on fifty-one. I don't know what else I can do. I've already tried and tested nearly everything in our house.

I click through some more London beauty blogs. I pause, looking at one blogger's photo of some Shoreditch street art. It looks like something you'd see on Flickr.

*Hmm, I wonder . . .*

I type 'Shoreditch street art' into Flickr images. A flurry of East London shots pop up on my page. They look seriously cool. If only I'd been there. If only I could have taken these images. My blog would look great.

I click on one of the images and notice a tiny 'C' with a score through the middle of it, with 'public domain' written underneath. Wait a minute – does that mean I can use this image for my blog?

I read the blurb. From what I can see . . . yes.

Within minutes I have a bank of free images from London – market food, street art, even some touristy-looking shots from Buckingham Palace.

With trembling fingers, I upload them to a new blog page. Keeping Lily's blog open beside mine, I start writing:

*Wonderful day out with my friends in London! You all have to try these locally sourced fruits – they're delicious, truly divine. Had to take a snap to share with you. I just couldn't help myself! Love IssaAdores xoxox*

I title the post 'Issa's London Escapade'. It looks like a really fun day out. My hand hovers over the publish button . . . I can't quite decide whether to publish it. I feel like I am crossing some invisible line.

But, I mean, I could easily have gone out and taken these photos. I could easily have visited these places. There's nothing weird about it – I will probably one day actually visit all of these spots. And then I can replace the photos with my own. They're just placeholders really.

With my mind set, I click publish and feel a surge of elation. My blog looks much cooler – much more like Lily's. I give it a couple of minutes and refresh the page. My follower count has already leaped up to fifty-three.